THE LAST DANCE IN AZTLAN

THE LAST DANCE IN AZTLAN

Grogan Ullah Khan

Writers Club Press
San Jose New York Lincoln Shanghai

The Last Dance in Aztlan

Writers Club Press
an imprint of iUniverse, Inc.

For information address:
iUniverse, Inc.
5220 S. 16th St., Suite 200
Lincoln, NE 68512
www.iuniverse.com

ISBN: 0-595-21980-2

Printed in the United States of America

To our three Kings: Modo, Kuku and Maxi.

O friends, O Chiapenec Otomis
    what's troubling you?

You're drunk with wine
    and sprawled on the ground?

Pick yourselves up, sober up
    and let's go home

      to our green spring land

Yes, come away from these dangers!

In the old days

wine was drunk in dangerous places
    of fire and flood

There jades were broken
    turquoise bracelets

    precious stones

    our children

    our princes who drank flower wine

Let's drink this wine
    this flower-spring water

In our flowering land
    our earth of flowers

In the place of rattlesnakes

Chiapas, our home
    the dew-flowers of life

    are sweet and fragrant

and nobility is glorified

In that land of plenty

sunflowers bloom

Friends! Can you hear?
    Let's go!

    Let's leave the chalk wine
        the flood-and fire wine

        of war!

    Let's go drink flower-dew wine

    in our land of flowers

Come, friends

listen to my song

 —Song 7

Mexico Shining: Songs of the Aztecs. Nancy Arbuthnot

Acknowledgements

Dangerous journeys should never be undertaken alone. The writing of this tale began several years ago, and spent several more years tucked away in my unconscious, haunting the dark waters of mind. In writing this story, I wish to thank my wife, first and foremost. I am also grateful to the following people for reading and commenting on the original manuscript: Dr. Michael Mahon, Dr. Joerg Salaquarda, and Don Stuefloten.

CHAPTER 1

Southernlands

The King of Toxcatl. There is nothing unusual about him. He has simply been chosen. It is his highest duty. It is his obligation. Declining the call is not part of his thought-pattern. What does he desire? The light. What does he love? Mankind. The cosmos. The warmth of the Sun.

Today they will come for him. They will adorn him as king. Four beautiful women shall serve as his consorts. He shall be in want of nothing. They shall praise his name above all men. Every knee shall bow before him. The palace shall be his. He shall be adorned with gold and jewels. His hair shall be scented; his body bathed and perfumed by his lovely maidens.

The earth turns. Its trajectory takes it around the Sun. Some planets circle faster. Some planets circle slower. Summer is followed by autumn. Autumn is followed by winter. Winter is followed by spring. Spring is followed by summer. He shall rise each day from his bed. He shall walk to the window and observe how the Sun and His warriors ascend the sky. He shall note the noonday when the Sun is greeted by the Valiant Women. As he stands gazing at the Sun, his heart shall be filled with longing. His consorts shall gently kiss his eyes, lips, and neck.

He shall not fear the night. He shall overcome the night. He shall awake and note the time. His passion shall go out to the priests who mercifully draw the precious blood from their ears.

The days shall pass. He shall wait patiently. His consorts shall continue to please him. At the end of the year he shall joyously and triumphantly greet his god.

Northernlands

Bad Palmen. There are neither palms nor springs in this desert mirage located in a barren valley between mountains. Even the grass is not real. People only pretend to play golf. Near cadavers simulate the gesticulations of twentysomethings. Twentysomethings replicate the cadavers. The shops are full of merchandise. No one buys anything. People sit in restaurants. But it is too hot to eat. Unheard ofs have perfect stars set in smooth and symmetrical concrete sidewalks. Everyone pretends to gape. No one looks. Moisture cools the skin. It is hot. Blistering hot. Everyone ignores the sun. It, too, does not really exist. Air conditioners grunt like marines in the war on reality.

Two Chicanas walk uneasily amongst the residents of Bad Palmen. They are wearing shorts and sneakers. Their sunglasses are mirrored. At first glance, they look like typical Americans. Only their car gives them away. They are driving an old Chevy. It belches smoke as fast as it does gas. It lacks both air conditioning and a paint job. But our girls are not envious. They have been to Bad Palmen. They have spent a night in a fabulous hotel, dined on lobster, and drank margaritas. They have even flirted with wealthy bachelors.

As they ascend upwards from the basin, and drive past surreal wind generators while listening to the beat of War, they know they shall soon be home. Santa Ana is only an hour or two away.

The driver depresses the accelerator. The mighty V-8 roars. The girls laugh. The speed increases. A truck stop comes into view. Dinosaurs rise out of the sand. Factory outlets appear. A bullet-ridden sign reminds them that an old Indian reservation borders the freeway. A strange feeling of sadness tugs at them. Distant memories? A casino beckons. They are not old enough, yet. Instinctively, they know that they shall one day gamble. It is in their blood.

They have not gone far. Already the old Chevy needs gas. How far is it to the next station? Stagecoach City appears. Eight exits.

The sun is hot. Too hot to get gas. Soft skin wrinkles quickly in the dry heat. They do not have air conditioning. The temperature is close to 120°F. The mountains have not yet cast their shadows. Stagecoach City stands alone. Unprotected. They take the first exit. A gas station, America, announces in neon lit signs that it also sells thirst busters. The old Chevy pulls into the station.

Southernlands

Lakeside. A young man, Tez, was walking along the lake. The wind blew. He breathed in deeply, taking in the scent of fertility, of the lush jungle, which had mixed with the lake's brine. Several birds, screeching, flew overhead. He reached down and picked up a smooth stone, rubbing it between his hands, and then hurling it out at the lake's surface. Tez watched curiously as it skipped twice and then sunk. The Sun was overhead. The wind swirled. It changed direction. His skin tingled. Off in the distance, he spotted another person walking towards him. His body began to tense. He had not seen his brother for several years. As they neared each other, they both stopped and stared. Their eyes scanned each other's now grown bodies, looking for signs of familiarity. Memories stirred from deep within. Galloping towards each other, they fell into each other's embrace, their joy overwhelming them.

The last time they had met, Tez had defeated his brother at patolli, a game of dice. Quetz had promised that when he returns from the monastery, where he is studying to be a priest, he would take revenge.

Throwing each other to the ground, they tested their own strength against the other. The sand scratched their bodies. Tez found himself in a headlock.

"I'm gonna make you eat sand," his older brother shouted, rubbing his knuckles into Ted's scalp.

Tez turned and struggled. His ears burned from his brother's powerful forearm. Slowly, he managed to wrench free from the other's grasp, almost tearing off his left ear in the process. Entwined, they rolled toward the water's edge. Tez fought to stand up. His brother, Quetz, lunged at him, knocking Tez backwards. Quetz lunged again, the force of his motion sailing him past Tez. Like a young cat, he landed in the shallow water. Springing to his feet, he caught a glimpse of his reflection in the still water. Mud covered his face. The Sun's reflection blinded him. Now Tez was upon him. The two rolled in the surf. Each one attempted to hold the other's head underwater. Was it a battle to the death? Or were they engaged in play?

They emerged salty and wet, laughing as they lay exhausted in the water. Quetz seemed the stronger. Reaching out, he gave Tez a strong but playful push to the chest, toppling him over again. But Tez was not to be outdone. He was a cadet, trained to be fearless. His martial abilities were becoming skillful. He crawled forward. Quetz leaped up and, laughing so that his strength almost left him, half ran—half stumbled—towards the beach. Tez pursued him. Regaining his strength, Quetz dashed down the beach. Tez followed. His brother's long fingernails had left gashes in his skin. Pumping with his arms and legs, he hoped to catch his adversary. He desired to prove his prowess. But Quetz was no easy quarry. He was fast. He had always been fast. The two raced for home.

※   ※   ※

At home. There was nothing unusual about their home. It was comfortable. They were not rich. Their father had always been able to provide them with a fair standard of living. It had been some time since the family had been reunited. Tez and Quetz were sitting opposite each other. Mother interrupted her cooking to bring out the *patolli* set. The boys eyed each other. Each felt certain of his chances. Quetz rubbed his hands together. Tez laughed and offered an insult. Mother enjoyed watching the mounting competition.

Quetz was her oldest son. He had always been the more serious of the two. When it came to carrying water, or learning how to fish, he undertook it with diligence. Tez, however, could rarely concentrate. He was always getting into trouble, playing tricks on people, getting into fights with other boys, or teasing girls. Mother regretted that he had taken after his father. Luckily though, he hadn't been born under a bad sign, as everyone she knew had feared as his birth approached. Instead, the day he had entered the world the diviner determined that he would become a warrior. Quetz, on the other hand, had always displayed a great intellectual interest. He loved all cultural pursuits: poetry; music; and astronomy most of all. Several years ago they had taken him to the *calmecac*, where he is studying to be a priest. She was proud of both of her boys.

The pieces were set and the boys readied themselves to play. Tez made the first move. Quetz hesitated. Instead of directly taking his turn, he decided to explain to Tez the esoteric meaning of the game, knowing that a lecture would stir his younger brother's ire, and perhaps break his concentration.

"I guess they didn't teach you that the fifty-two squares on the board represent the number of years in the solar cycle, did they?"

"Why don't you go ahead and move, big brother, or I'll move for you."

Quetz moved his bean.

"Do you know why we race through the squares—only to end up on the very same square that we had started from? Time, little brother. Time. But I guess they don't teach you about time at the telpochcalli, do they?"

Tez squinted at his brother, and then whispered:

"Quetz? Do you know what it's like to hold a girl in your arms, to feel her warmth, to run your hands over her smooth body, to nibble on her sweet mangos? I guess they don't teach you about that at the *calmecac*, do they?"

The boys' eyes locked. Tension mounted. Tez's right hand unconsciously formed a fist. Quetz's fingers, with their long nails, stretched taut into a claw. If only they were out in the open, on the beach, where they could lunge at each other, kicking, punching, biting, scratching! Then Quetz laughed. Tez, too, broke a smile. They both sensed that nothing would be solved—at least not today.

A shadow suddenly appeared in the room. Both boys froze. Mother jumped up. A slight wind blew through the room; then it was gone.

The forest. The sun had already set. Most people were hurrying home. The boys had spoken with the neighbor girls. They had talked them into taking a long early evening stroll. They had known each other since infancy. Naturally, and rightfully, the girls were frightened. Evil creatures roamed about at night. Malicious dwarves inhabited the forests. Headless monsters stumbled on the roads. Decapitated heads rested and laughed hauntingly from the top of rocks and boulders. And above all, the feared goddesses of the night waited at the crossroads, hoping to strike unwary travelers with paralysis. But the boys were not frightened. Since infancy they had accompanied their father on nocturnal journeys. He had taught them how to avoid danger and ward off evil, and the girls knew this.

They came to a clearing in the forest. Tez's passion had kindled into a warm fire. He was torn between his physical attraction to Quiauhxochitl (rain-flower), who constantly drove him mad with the way she tossed her mane, and Atototl's (water-bird) spirit, her sense of being lost, of introversion. He wanted to lie with both of them.

Quetz had strayed a few yards from the group. He seated himself on a log and looked up at the sky. Matlalxochitl (green flower), named after the color of her cat like eyes, joined him. Quetz hardly noticed her. She had always been in love with him, and had been terribly hurt when he had joined the priesthood. As young children they had often played by the stream together. From where she was standing, Atototl (water-bird) jealously observed Quetz and her friend, Matlalxochitl (green flower). She had imagined that Quetz would one day be her man. Since he had left for the *calmecac*, she had become unusually rotund. Many of the older men were beginning to find her voluptuous. She was slightly self-conscious and often sought to hide her swollen bosom behind her crossed arms.

Without warning, Quetz jumped up from the log. His action startled everyone. He was staring at the sky. The others joined him.

"What's wrong?" Atototl whispered, her voice barely rising above the breeze.

The evening noises of the forest were becoming perceptively louder. Fearing something terrible, they instinctively huddled closer together. Tez looked around. Reaching down, he picked up a stick and took out an amulet.

"Look at the sky!" Quetz commanded, his voice stern but creaking against mounting darkness.

"I don't see anything," Tez replied, after a few moments.

"I don't either," Quiauhxochitl (rain-flower) added, wrapping her arm in Tez's.

"You're not *looking!*" Quetz almost shouted.

The group focused. Slowly, they noticed that something was in deed happening. The horizon was becoming darker. Ever so slowly, a crack appeared in the middle of the sky. It parted the stars, becoming brighter as they stared.

"What is it?" Tez asked.

"I don't know," Quetz replied. "I've never seen anything like it."

Continuing to gaze up at the now burning cosmic ear of corn, Quetz began shivering. Pulling out a knife, he drew blood from his ears. The girls helped collect the precious fluid.

Then the crack in the sky exploded into a conflagration, its flames leaping and dancing ominously. Quetz fell to the ground. Though his own strength had left him, Tez lifted his brother slowly.

The youngsters turned and wanted to flee. But the forest had become impregnable. They could sense the evil—the malice—that wanted to enshroud them. Tez gathered some wood and started a fire. The night continued to draw in about them. The celestial holocaust raged on. They lit branches and held them up as weapons, warding off the darkness. The two boys repeated a secret incantation their father had taught them long ago. A dark shadow appeared in the fire, dancing amongst the flames, forming itself from the heat. Tez understood and sighed with relief. The fire crackled, spitting and hissing at the gathered group. Flames jumped above their heads. The shadow continued to grow, taking on shape.

The father they had never completely trusted stepped from out of the fire. Embracing his two sons in his powerful arms, and acknowledging the girls, his mere presence immediately quelled their fear.

"Father? What is it?" Quetz asked, pointing at the sky.

"An omen. Ominous. We shall soon know its meaning. The roads are troubled. I have secured a path for you to go home. Do *not* stray from my path." And as quickly as he had appeared, he vanished.

Tez led the way. Quetz brought up the rear. Silently, and in single file, they followed their father's path.

☙   ☙   ☙

The marketplace. Few people noticed the five friends when they entered the marketplace on their way home. The streets were crowded with people. Everyone was pointing up at the sky. Diviners stood pondering its significance. A heavy drumbeat could be heard. The priests were busy sacrificing.

Their mother met them before their home. Her face was pale. She, too, had spoken with her husband. She was glad to see that they had returned safely.

It was doubtful that anyone would sleep that night. Quetz hugged his family and hurriedly returned to the monastery where he hoped to be of some help. Tez lingered a bit longer in the marketplace, listening to the gossip, and exchanging opinions with other cadets, before walking the three girls home.

Northernlands

Stagecoach City. Everything is gray. It has not been green for months, if it had ever been. No one pretends to play golf. Plastic palms have not been planted. The streets are deserted. The wind blows continuously. It is hot. Terribly hot. The mountains are grayish brown. There are no trees in Stagecoach City. Tumbleweeds roll down the deserted streets. They collect in abandoned yards. No one removes them. No one seems to notice. Nothing else moves.

The two girls have stopped to get gas. The old gray Chevy is down to empty. Masha steps out of the car. She is covered with perspiration. She fumbles through her pockets for money. Her short hair is an asset in the heat. She walks towards the window, turns, and asks her sister if she wants a coke. Mina leans forward and nods, the skin of her back pealing off of the vinyl upholstery. It is too hot to talk. Mina looks around. Heat waves rise from the street.

Masha returns. She hands Mina the can of soda. She does not open it. Instead, she pulls back her ponytail and places the cold can against her neck. The sensation of cool penetrates her skin, sending a message of relief to her numbed brain. She rubs the can over her forehead and face. Masha takes the hose and inserts the nozzle. She flips up the switch and the gas begins to flow into the tank, pulsating with each gallon. Mina stares ahead, her gaze unfocused, her mind still blank.

The shopping center across the street is almost abandoned. The old pharmacy has long since closed, its windows peppered by young boys with air pistols and slingshots. The heat waves continue to rise. Sweat fills Mina's eyes. It is hard to see. One shop is open. She rubs the sweat from her eyes, trying not to disturb her sunglasses. Her eyes ache. A neon sign stands above the shop. Are its lights on? Or have they been overwhelmed by the sun's brilliance? The barely visible sign reads *Studio Mictlan*. A large high-heeled shoe, a spiked shoe, a knife jutting from its sole, a shoe barely perceptible against the glare, stands above the studio's sign.

Several tumbleweeds roll past. The wind does not cool. It is hot. Mina continues to stare at the sign. She cannot look away. The words, *Studio Mictlan*, whisper to her, enchanting her.

Masha holds the nozzle and stares off at the mountains. Her mind, too, is blank. The handle clicks. She hears the door open, but does not look over. She returns the hose and closes the tank. The car door is open. She takes a sip from her soda and looks around. Sweat fills her eyes. The sun is bright. Mina is crossing the street. It is too hot to wonder. It is even too hot to care.

The studio. The air conditioner is never turned off. Inside, it is cool. Ted emerges from the darkroom. He studies the prints. A young Hmong couple is dressed in traditional costumes. Palm trees and ferns provide the setting. They look happy. An older Hmong woman is sitting on the chair, her feet dangling several inches above the floor. She looks pleased. Ted hands them the print. The old woman says something in Hmong. The young man answers. The woman laughs.

An Anglo family of four is impatiently waiting their turn. The woman is trying on a Civil War era gown. The man is debating with himself whether he looks better as a Yankee or a Confederate general. Both are standing in front of mirrors. Ted watches them, his index finger gently caressing the top of his camera. Their children are busy dressing as well. Like their father, they can't decide whether they should be cowboys or Indians.

The door opens. Ted does not look up. His gaze is now fixed on the camera. A burst of hot air fills the room. The air conditioner groans. Ted reaches over and flips on the fan. The door has not been completely closed. He looks up. A woman, drenched in sweat, is standing at the entrance. She does not move. She does not look around.

The studio is dark. Mina cannot see. Slowly, her eyes begin to adjust. Figures and outfits come into view. Costumes fill open closets. A man, thin, sharp features, dark eyes, pale—as if the blood had been drained from him years ago—stares at her. The Hmong family exits. They close the door. General Lee notices her. A cowboy is shooting an Indian. Scarlet O'Hara looks over.

Mina's eyes are still full of sweat. Her white cotton T-shirt clings to her body. Ted notices her breasts. His eyes follow her figure. She is wearing shorts and tennis shoes. Her legs are becoming. Her ankles look slightly swollen. Has she twisted them?

She moves towards the counter. Her shoes squeak like mice.

Scarlet advances. They are ready. Ted motions for the stranger to wait.

He resets the background. The Anglo family poses. Cameras begin to click. Mina watches. She does not move.

✿

CHAPTER 2

Northernlands

At the studio.

She steps into *Studio Mictlan.*

"Can I help you?" Ted asks.

"I—ah—my sister and I—we were just coming back from Bad Palmen."

"Most people are either going to or coming from Bad Palmen."

"This is really neat. I didn't even know this place exists."

"How can I help you?"

"Wait—let me get my sister." She looks out the window.

"She does that sometimes."

"Does what?" he asks, leaning on a wall, crossing his ankles.

"Drives off and leaves me when I wander off."

"Do you wander off very often? There's a Greyhound station not far from here, if you need to get home."

"So like, I'm supposed to pick out a costume and then you're gonna photograph me?"

"So—what were you doing in Bad Palmen?" he asks, leading her to the woman's wardrobe. She begins looking through the costumes.

Ted studies her body. He considers her. It is almost closing time. Is she worth it? Perhaps, he muses.

"How would I look in this one?" she asks, holding up a Victorian era gown.

"Green is definitely you." He looks at her shoes. "First, we've got to get rid of those sneakers."

"Why? Why do you keep this place so dark?"

"Why? They don't fit. Here, try these on." He hands her a pair of shin high lace boots.

"I hate boots. Where can I change?"

"There's a wardrobe over there. It's big enough for you to change in."

"A wardrobe? Like in—ah—Narnia, right? You know, that place…"

"Right over there," he says, smiling.

She changes and then reenters the room. Ted has set up the Victorian era background. Loading the camera, he sets it onto a tripod.

"I'm going to take three pictures of you. The first is with a Polaroid."

"A Polaroid?"

"For you and your friends. Plus, it'll give you an idea of where we're going. Then, I'm going to use an old-fashioned pin holed camera. Black and white. So it'll look authentic. Then we'll do a newer color photograph. How does that sound?"

"Sounds great. Where do I stand? Oh yeah, what about digital?"

"We'll see." He studies her face.

"How old are you?"

"Almost eighteen. I just graduated. That's why we were in Bad Palmen."

"Graduation present?"

Her face is marked with acne. Blemished. He feels sorry for her. Underneath all that acne, she could be lovely. He wonders if her self-esteem has suffered as a result? He also wonders if she has ever known a man? An image of her in the back seat of a car, parked on top of a hill, overlooking the city, necking, comes to mind. He dismisses the image and walks towards her.

"I want this to be real nice for you. Is this your first time?"

"Yes."

He holds up a mirror for her to see her face.

"Sit down. Right here," he commands. She continues standing.

"Your make-up is too heavy."

She puts the mirror down and looks away. Shame, and then anger, well up inside of her.

"I mean, for that era."

He takes out some make-up remover and, using cotton balls, begins removing it from her face. Her body is tense. She looks to the side. He continues. The cotton balls are dark. He throws them into a waste paper basket. Her skin is exposed. Unprotected. She feels vulnerable and slightly leans back on her heels.

"Why don't you sit down over here?"

He leads her to a vanity mirror. She is both amused and excited by the mirror. When she sees herself, she looks away. He draws her gaze back to the mirror. He takes out a small black leather case with gold hinges from the upper drawer. The name Estee Lauder is engraved on the front of the case.

"Estee Lauder?" she asks, bewildered.

"Or would you prefer some other brand? Lancome? Yves Rocher?"

"Estee Lauder's fine."

He opens the case and takes out a jar of moisturizing cream. Despite his age and gender, his hands are smooth, undisturbed by hard work. The tips of his long, piano player like fingers, dip into the cream. Gently, he touches her face. She closes her eyes as the cool smooth cream contacts her skin. He moves his fingers in tiny circles over her cheeks and forehead. She suppresses a smile.

Closing the jar and returning it to its case, he takes out a concealing stick. It is firm, yet he is gentle. Underneath his care, her scars begin to disappear. Before applying the powder blush—candlelit rose—he sponges an illuminating foundation onto her. Finally, using a long brush, he dusts her with a translucent loose powder. She opens her eyes and smiles.

"We're not done yet," he warns.

He closes her eyes with the palm of his hand. His finger traces her eyes, probing her bone structure. Quickly, like an experienced artisan, he takes up the pencil and applies the eyeliner, and then, changing tools, the brow definer. Finally, he does her eyelashes. She opens her eyes.

His index finger touches her lips. He traces their outline, probing their inner fold. Opening the lipstick container, and rotating it so that it rises above its sheath, he touches it to her puckered and then stretched lips.

He takes her by the hand and leads her to a chair. Her hair is not quite right. He removes the pins, allowing it to fall, and then resets it in a proper bun. He steps back.

The cheap Polaroid flashes brightly. Quickly, he moves to the tripod and the old handmade camera flashes. There is a burst of light. She is blinded. She cannot see. Before she can recover, he is on his knees. The 35mm Zeiss is aimed and fired. She is bathed in light. Flashes, bursts, surround her. She cannot move. She does not know where he is. He is over and under her, at once on the floor and overhead. Her mind is blank. Then she sees—a rose. The bursts of light continue. When they finally cease, it is night.

Walking home. It is dark. The sun is gone. There is no moon. The wind is blowing in from the desert. Stagecoach City does not have street lamps. The library is still open. It is a small library. Ted enters the library and goes to the new books section. He has read almost everything the town has to offer.

Two new works on cockroaches sit on the shelf. Ted pages through both of them, enjoying the pictures, and then carries them to the checkout counter.

It is dark. Young toughs, gangsters, hang around. Latino youths sit on the hoods of their cars. Most are wearing white T-shirts, long slacks, tennis shoes and bandanas. Ted walks past them. They know him. No one addresses him. He continues walking. Several black youths are leaning against a fence. They are wearing oversized football jerseys. Ted does not make eye contact with them. He continues. Approaching the end of the block, he nears a funeral parlor. Several Hmong youths are loitering about. They address him. He nods. He crosses the street and continues walking.

He passes a house. The yard, like all yards in Stagecoach City, has not been kept up. The garage has been blackened by fire. An old car sits in it. A young white couple is on the porch. They appear drunk.

He passes another house. It looks abandoned. That, too, is not unusual. An old black Lab is chained to a tree. There is no meat on him. His eyes look vacant. He does not see Ted as he walks past. The dog stands and turns. Is he oblivious to the heavy chain? Has he been pulling it for so many years that he no longer realizes its existence? Ted looks at the Lab. His hind legs are crippled with arthritis. Ted turns the corner and approaches an old run down apartment complex. There is only one tenant. He walks up to the door and rings the bell.

"Ted! Come in." Her hair is in curlers. She isn't wearing any makeup. Her stretch pants barely cover her enormous waist. In fact, a bit of pink colored skin, tattooed with stretch marks, protrudes from the crack between her pants and her top.

"Dite," Ted says, hugging her. His arms cannot reach around her shoulders.

"Do you wanna sit down?" There is clutter everywhere.

"No, thanks," he politely says, noticing the scent of cough syrup on her breath.

"You look bad, Dite. You look like shit."

"I know, Ted." She begins to cry.

"But I didn't know you'd be stoppin' by today," she sobs.

"Dite. You shouldn't do it for me. It's for you. Isn't that what I've taught you?"

"That's what you always said, Ted."

"How long's it been since you've been out of here?"

"I don't know. I've lost track. Please don't look around." Unwashed dishes are stacked in the sink. Old pieces of gnawed and rancid steak bone lie on the counter. Ted walks over and opens a window. Hot desert air blows in.

It has been almost six months since Ted met Dite. She wandered into his studio for no apparent reason.

"Why haven't you been to the studio lately?"

"I don't know. I just haven't had time."

"Bullshit Dite! There's a reason for everything, right? *You* decided to come to my studio. *You* sought me out. Now…"

"Okay. You don't have to get so nasty about it."

"Dite. Have I ever been mean to you? Now, I want you to go to the studio as soon as possible. Okay?"

"All right."

Ted hugs her and leaves the complex. He recalls the first time he saw her. She must have weighed four hundred pounds. She still weighs four hundred pounds. He saw her walking, T-shirt pulled up, stretch-marked gut hanging out, rosy cheeked, barefoot, thumping to the store. His eyes had followed her. She looked defiant, hostile, and paradoxically shy and ashamed all at the same time. He hadn't expected that one day she would walk into his studio. She claimed that she was an artist. Thus far, he still has not unraveled the nature of her art.

He stops in front of his house. The chain link gate is closed. The ivy has grown up around the house, forming a crown. His Ford van is parked in the driveway. It is covered with sand. He does not open the gate. He looks around. Across from his house is an open field that usually catches fire and burns during the Santa Ana winds. Beyond the field is the Indian reservation. There are several fences between him and the Indians. He looks back at his house. Behind the van and against the wall is an old motorcycle, a 1962 white four stroke Triumph 650. It has been modified for the dirt, for hill climbing. It is his pride and joy. A machine made at the height of British power, before all the plastic two-stroke rice burners hit the market. "Goddamn crotch rockets," he curses to himself. "Nothing can compare," he assures himself, "not even a Harley."

Several small shadows are moving about in the house. A blue light is on in the living room. They are not expecting him. He rarely sleeps at home. Someone enters the kitchen. It is her. Sounds of the blender and the garbage disposer travel towards him. He does not enter. Instead, he places an envelope in the mailbox and leaves, walking back to the studio.

Southernlands

At the canal. Helping Atototl (water bird) into the canoe, Tez paddled vigorously. He wanted to do a little fishing and show her some of the new *chinampas* that had recently been constructed. The canals were busy. It was impossible to speed. Many people, merchants, artisans and farmers, were busy transporting their goods to the market. Tez looked back at Atototl and smiled. She returned his smile and reassured him that they were making good time.

The canals were not wide. He maneuvered their canoe skillfully. Other youths shouted teases at them. The canal's banks floated gently past. Atototl's mind took in the sound of the paddle splashing in the water. Leaning back, she let the Sun bathe her face. Tez smiled and self-consciously looked away.

Tez felt Atototl stiffen. He looked up. Several kids were pointing. Boats all along the canal began to stop. It was impossible to go on.

Tez and Atototl looked at each other, bewildered. Someone shouted something indiscernible. Their stomachs tightened.

They smelled it before they actually saw it. Smoke. Something was on fire—or was going to catch on fire. Many people abandoned their boats and began running towards the city. Tez turned the canoe and paddled. His shoulder muscles bulged. Sweat formed on his brow. They gained speed. An abandoned canoe drifted into their path—*thud!* The crash spilled both of them into the water. They fought to hold on to each other. The current was strong. The water came in from the mainland. Several people, extending polls to them, pulled them to safety.

Water dripped from their near naked bodies. Tez motioned to Atototl. They both stared at the plume, which now rose maliciously over the city. People were running in the direction of the smoke. They were both young and strong. Easily overtaking many, they neared the source.

They entered the inner city. The smoke rose like a dark serpent, blocking the Sun. Their lungs hurt. Men and women were frantically carrying pales of water. Someone handed them several large heavy jugs. They continued running towards the smoke.

Turning a corner, they entered the main street. Their arms ached from the strain of the jugs. The temple rose above them. Its pinnacle reached up towards the heavens, bigger than any mountain. Flames leaped from the top. They handed their jugs to a young priest who bounded up the steps of the pyramid.

Scores of priests huddled off to the side. Most had been badly burned. Doctors and diviners ran past Tez and Atototl towards the injured. Rising ever higher, the serpent cloud continued to threaten. Fire hissed and spat. Heaven and earth met. Smoke choked their lungs and brought tears to their eyes. They moved slowly towards the injured.

Wounded priests were either seated or lying on the ground. Doctors were applying salves and bandages. Atototl grabbed Tez by his

shoulders and spun him with surprising force. "Quetz!"
shouted.

No one was aiding him. They ran towards him. He acknowledged
their presence with his eyes. His severely blistered hand communicated his pain. The skin had peeled off, revealing the inner pink
flesh. They knelt down beside him. Atototl stroked his head. Taking
hold of his forearm, she gently raised it up and away from them. Tez
dropped to his knees and took out his member. Pointing it at his
brother's burned hand, he closed his eyes and relaxed. Warm urine
began to flow and bathe the wound. A doctor approached. Taking
Quetz's arm and motioning for the two to step back, he smeared
Quetz's hand with a sweet salve, bandaged it and then moved on.

The serpent continued to rise and hiss above the city. Everywhere,
priests, despaired and dejected, fought to oppose the flames. The
Sun struggled to shine through the thick black plume. Night
descended onto Tenochtitlan.

❦   ❦   ❦

At home. The family sat and ate the simple corn and tomato meal
mother had prepared. The atmosphere was solemn. Quetz held his
bandaged hand on his lap. He had not returned to the monastery in
weeks. Father had not said a word since dinner began. Yesterday,
lightning struck the Temple Xiuhtecuhtli without emitting thunder.
Fear and trepidation were mounting in the land.

"Three have appeared, five more shall be," Father finally said,
without looking up from his food.

Quetz and Tez stopped eating and stared at him, waiting.

"What are they?" Tez asked.

Refusing to respond, Father continued eating. Mother walked
across the floor and sat down next to him.

"Tell us," she pleaded, placing her hand on his leg.

After some hesitation, he began again: "Soon, another stream of
fire shall appear in the sky. It shall be divided into three parts and

give off sparks. Then the lake shall boil. The waters shall rise up and destroy many houses. You shall hear a woman crying out: 'My children, we must run from this city!' You will look in vain, but you shall not find her. Fishermen shall catch a strange sea-beast in their nets. It shall have a mirror in its head. The mirror shall reveal strange creatures riding on deer and marching in ranks. And terrible two-headed monsters, the Monsters of the Twilight, shall appear on the streets and devour whomever they find. Take heed!"

Quetz turned a ghostly pale. Standing up slowly, and steadying himself against an onrush of lightheadedness, he walked to the window and searched through the dark haze for the temple. Mother's eyes fixed on a spot on the floor. Tez, sitting cross-legged, took hold of his feet.

"When shall all these things happen?" Quetz asked, turning to his Father.

"Am I a diviner? Do I spend my time reading the *tonalpoualli*? I am a wizard! Not a priest!"

Quetz looked hurt. His Father rarely voiced his disdain for priests, but when he did, it was unmistakable.

Mother slowly responded to a determined knock at the door. Her strain remained hidden as a small, crooked, elfish-like woman crept past her and, without so much as a word, sat down next to Father. Mother moved next to Tez. No one greeted the small coal eyed woman.

"What will happen to us?" Tez asked, fearfully.

The room began to darken. The elfish woman looked over at Father, who had begun to brood. The room continued to darken. Mother hugged herself. The cruel elf smirked, seeming to enjoy the way dark rings began to appear under Father's eyes, anticipating that soon something darker than a shadow will emanate forth from him. Mother knew that he was locked in a struggle, wanting to contain his power—his wrath. Quetz and Tez were too old to be cowed. Quetz stiffened and faced his Father. Tez refused to take his question back. The shadow passed. Father sighed.

"Haven't I taught you boys anything? Have you not learned where power resides?"

Purposefully ignoring the crippled hand, his eyes fell on his eldest son, Quetz. Then he darted a hard glance at Tez.

"Power—perhaps you shall one day experience it. We shall see."

Standing up, Father walked to the door. The elvish woman followed. Quetz and Tez held each other's eyes as Mother began cleaning up.

At the temple courtyard. The preparations were already under way for the next great fiesta. The planning committee was just in the process of completing the selection of the honored women that would have the privilege of grinding the seeds, adorning the god, and marshaling the dancers.

Tez hoped to be selected to dance at the next fiesta. He had often watched how the brave warriors, dancing in long processions, went on for hours, never stopping, not even to urinate. To fall out of line was a dishonor. The women, using twitches as whips, kept the men going. It was a wonderful occasion—a time to celebrate the great god, *Huitzilopochtli.*

If he were chosen to dance, though, he would have to dance at the back. He had never captured an opponent, though he looked forward to the chance.

Today was Market Day. Crowds were already gathering in the early morning light. He hoped to run across someone he knew. He walked aimlessly about for several hours, past stands of fruit, vegetables, meats, spices, precious stones, beautiful quetzal feathers, and artisans selling their crafts. He even passed the slave market and inspected some of the latest slaves: bankrupt gamblers and people caught from outlying regions. He dreamed of war and couldn't wait to get back to school, where he could continue studying its art.

Finally, the priests had made their decision. They had selected the new King of Toxcatl. Tez pushed to the front of the crowd, hoping to get a glimpse of the fortuitous young man.

The crowd continued to swell, generating ever more excitement as their numbers rose. The young slender but muscular man finally appeared to a loud murmur in the crowd, which was quickly followed by hoots of acceptance. Everyone was in awe as he was crowned with quetzal feathers and adorned in the finest feathers and jewels. Tez longed to be so honored. But he was a warrior, he reminded himself. Four lovely young women, also beautifully dressed in feathers, gold and jade, took their places next to the King, placing their hands on his body. Priests began beating drums. With an old priest leading the way, the King and his consorts followed. The crowd separated respectfully to allow them to pass. The drumbeats intensified. Tez followed the procession for a while and then lost them in the throng.

Northernlands

At the studio. The air conditioner groans to keep the studio cool. Outside, it is hot. Ferociously hot. Ted hasn't had a customer all day. He is sitting at a desk, plucking at an old manual typewriter. It is almost noon. He takes a drink of distilled water and continues typing. Tibetan prayer bells clang. The door opens. A woman walks in.

"Ted?"

It is Dite. She has walked to the studio. The heat has caused her mascara to run. Her puffy cheeks are lined by black streaks.

"Ted?"

He types the last sentence and then carefully places his manuscript in a drawer, locking it.

"Dite. Glad you could make it."

"It's nice and cool in here. Do you have anything to drink?"

"You know where the Fridge is."

Ted gathers his camera and sets the scene. Dite finishes her diet soda and then goes to the wardrobe. She knows which outfit to choose. When she reenters the room she is wearing only a long flowing silk skirt, which Ted has created for her. Her huge swollen breasts hang down, hovering just above her navel. She attempts to walk softly to prevent her body from shaking. Ted motions for her to move onto the platform. A painting of the ocean's surf looms in the background. The waves are wild. There is driftwood. Dite walks over to the large swan prop and places her right hand on its long neck. Ted walks towards her, angry that her hair is not right. Adjusting it, he walks back and points his camera. He is not pleased with the shot. He returns and, taking out bright red lipstick, does her lips. He places her hair in a bun. Still, he is not happy. Removing the swan, he asks her to sit down. The scene is incorrect. He is not sure why. He replaces the ocean with a black background.

Ted walks back to the wardrobe. When he returns, he is carrying a leather girdle with nine holes cut in both the front and back. Handing Dite the girdle, he moves behind her and cinches it closed. Three, five, seven, nine protrusions of fat appear through the girdle. Taking the lipstick in hand, he paints nipples onto her bulging rolls of fat. Each roll is transformed into a breast. He slowly strokes each one, fondling them gently, kissing them. Kneeling before her, he smiles. Her pale pinkish white body hangs in space. The camera clicks. Flashes of light engulf her.

Outside, it is hot. Terribly hot.

Southernlands

At the forest. Clouds lined the sky. Patches of blue intermittently shone through. The forest itself looked as though the intense green they had known and loved was graying.

Tez led the way, following a path he had discovered only several weeks ago. Atototl (water bird) and Quiauhxochitl (rain-flower) followed at a close distance. The humidity was intense. They could sense each other's presence. As they brushed up against each other, their perspiration mingled. Their scents pleasantly filled each other's nostrils. Quetz and Matlalxochitl (green-flower) hurried to catch their three friends.

Tez led them to a large stone. The five gathered around it. Atototl giggled. Quiauhxochitl pinched Tez's ribs. He smiled and leaned away. Quetz, looking serious, put a stop to their play.

Overhead, the sky continued to gray. Several birds looked on from their perches. Matlalxochitl, kissing Tez's forehead, placed feathers upon his head. Atototl, kissing his lips, and placing her hands on his chest, gently pushed him onto the rock. He did not resist. Quiauhxochitl, kissing each eye, reassured him that all would be well. His arms and legs dangled. He felt the rock's bone penetrating coldness. He looked up at the sky, searching for the Sun behind the gray.

The three young women took hold of his arms and legs. Atototl and Quiahxochitl had his arms. Matlalxochitl had both his feet. Still, he did not fight. His brother, taking out an obsidian knife, which had been carefully concealed in soft deer leather, slowly and reverently unwrapped it, allowing the Sun's light to shine upon it. Holding the knife overhead, he chanted a few sacred incantations. Ceremoniously, he presented it to the four directions, holding it with both his good left hand and his badly burned hand.

Quiauhxochitl leaned over and kissed Tez's chest. Atototl did the same. Quetz approached. His face had become paler. He loved his brother deeply. Tez steadied himself. His eyes traveled from one girl to the other. Their happiness calmed him. Quetz stood over him. He rested the knife on his brother's chest. Tez felt it. His skin tingled beneath it. Quetz leaned over and stared deep into Tez's soul. Tez's look told him that he was ready. Picking up the knife, he made a quick skillful incision in the skin above his heart. Tez focused on the sky. The three girls tightened their grip on his ankles and wrists. Warm precious fluid quickly turned from a trickle to a flow. Quetz cut again. Tez's torso was now bathed in blood. Atototl and Quiau-hxochitl placed flowers over the wound on his chest. A deep silence blanketed the group for some time. Suddenly, they released their grips. Quetz grabbed his brother and embraced him. The others joined them. Tears streamed. Overflowing joy rose from them and galloped forth.

Northernlands

At the studio. It is hot and gray, yet she returns. The freeways, as usual, are jammed. Cars move senselessly in and out of lanes and then vanish. People fume and then disappear. Carbon dioxide rises. Eyes burn. No one progresses. Aggression looms. Anonymity. No humans are visible. Angles prohibit eye contact. Cold steel. Triggers cocked. The old Chevy inches along the concrete canal.

He is sitting alone in his studio. The typewriter is idle. The top drawer of his desk remains locked. He strums his guitar. Memories of Santa Cruz and Vietnam come to mind and co-mingle. Old songs he had composed long ago for forgotten conquests. The faces blur. Was she blond or brunette? Blue eyes or brown? Does it matter? The song remains. The cliffs, the sea, the surf, the jungle—all continue to exist. "No amount of napalm could ever vanquish jungle and surf," he says aloud to himself.

Outside the studio an old woman has taken up her guard post. Those who pass her pretend not to notice her. She is defiant. The world is her enemy. Her weapon: the Bible. Her proclamation: *The end of the world!* She enters the studio and asks Ted for a glass of water. He obliges. "Have you read Revelation?" she inquires. He nods and continues strumming.

The highway narrows into two lanes. Road signs only whisper of Stagecoach City's existence. The old Chevy rises out of the stale smog of Los Angeles, the city of angels. At the top, a breeze greets her. The barren hills go unnoticed. Rays like daggers stab at the sides of her eyes, slipping the defenses of her mirrored sunglasses. Her eyes ache.

The door clangs. She enters. Light streams into the studio. He does not look up.

"I've written a song for you," he says.

She looks at him, credulously. But she is young.

"I lost an earring. I think I lost it here."

He continues playing. Still, he has not looked up. She listens to the guitar's folksy 60's style ballad. She watches his nimble fingers move from string to string.

"I said, I think I lost an earring here. I liked the pictures."

"Look around for it, if you want. I haven't seen it," he says, ignoring her.

She wanders about the studio, inspecting the costumes, masks and figures. She finds a photo album and begins thumbing through it.

Ted sets his instrument down and peers at her.

"You could make an excellent model. I was really surprised by the photos. But, there was something missing—from a professional point of view."

"What do you mean?"

"From a strictly professional perspective, of course. Have you ever thought about attending a modeling school?"

She sits down, self-conscious. Ted turns up both the air conditioner and the fan. Dust blows across the room and then settles.

"Have you ever considered it? Like...?"

"Modeling school? I was never pretty enough," she says, ashamedly. "Besides, they're usually not looking for..." Her voice trails off.

"Nonsense. A good photographer, an artist, can take anyone and release their potential."

"What do you mean?"

"Do you know what's inside of you? No one knows until it's released. A photographer is like a guide, leading you to *yourself*, helping you to discover who you really are."

"Have you ever...?"

"Take a look at the album. What do you see?"

"I like this one."

"Why?"

"I don't know."

"That's what you have to discover. By the way, what have you read?" he asks.

"Not much."

"Not much? Kafka? Camus? Kerrouac? Hesse?"

"Who? I read a couple…"

"Someone your age should start by reading Hesse. Then…"

Their arms brush against each other. Sweat mingles. He takes her wrist and hands her two underlined cat-eared copies of *Demian* and *Siddhartha*. She stares at their covers.

"What does this have to do with modeling?"

"Discovering. It has to do with *discovering*. That's what modeling is. Will you read them?"

Her vision is glued to the books. He picks up the camera and, without shooting her, studies her through the lens. She stares at him, confused.

"I'd like to help you."

He pulls the trigger four or five times. She laughs.

"Discovering is serious. There's nothing funny about it." The camera continues to click. He moves around her, catching her profile, zooming in on her features.

"What are you going to do with all those pictures? Put them in your album?"

"No. Study them. You're not ready, yet."

The camera continues to mechanically click. The room has cooled. Mina pages through the books. Outside, the mountains begin to cast their shadows on the dry town of Stagecoach City. She leaves.

CHAPTER 3

❀

Northernlands

At the studio. The sun has not risen yet. It is still dark. The dawn air is pleasant, yet foreboding of the heat that is to come. Ted pulls into the parking lot. The old gray haired woman is already standing guard. He walks towards her.

"Good morning, Ted."

"Mornin'."

"Did you get a chance to read the latest issue I left in your studio?"

"Issue?"

"Magazine, my dear. *These End Times Revealed!*"

"Not yet."

"There's a lot in there I think you'd like."

Ted smiles and walks past her. He searches through his pockets until he finds his keys. The old woman continues speaking:

"It's all about the Book of Revelation. Have you ever read it?"

"Not in a long time. And I'm not sure that I—you're a Jehovah's Witness, aren't you? Or is it an Adventist? Baptist?"

"None of the above. I had an aunt who was a Witness. Knew the Pastor personally, she did. Used to even visit his pyramid every year. Went all the way out to Pennsylvania, she did. I've got cousins who are Adventists. My husband was Born Again. I heard someone in the family's a Mormon, somewhere out there in Utah. Got a niece, I hear, back east, who's a Brethern. I grew up Catholic. But now I'm a Dawn Truth Proclaimer, I am. We go strait back to our Lord, before there ever were any Jehovahs, Mormons, or, in heaven's name, what have you."

"I see," Ted says, unlocking the door and stepping into his studio.

The old woman follows, undeterred. Ted closes the door.

"I just wanted to share something from the Holy Scriptures with you."

Ted opens a canister and scoops out some coffee grounds.

"Would you like some?"

"Is it American?"

"Mexican, I believe."

"Too strong for my stomach. Revelation Chapter 9:3 reads: "And out of the smoke they came down upon the earth..."

"Are you sure you wouldn't like any coffee? I think I've got some instant."

"During those days men will seek death, but they will not find it; they will long to die, but death will elude them...That was verse 6."

"Would you like a cup of instant coffee?"

"A cup of tea would be lovely. English tea. Only English, mind you. How about Chapter 18:4?"

"Zenith? It is Zenith, right? Why don't you sit down?"

"I'm fine. 'Then I heard another voice from heaven say: 'Get out of her my people!'"

"Here you go. I hope it's OK."

"I'll just take it and go back outside. Thank you. Remember: *Babylon the Great has fallen!*"

"I'll keep that in mind," Ted sighs with relief, closing the door behind her.

※   ※   ※

At the studio. It is almost ten o'clock. The noonday sun is flexing its might. Inside, the air conditioner groans to ward off the heat. Outside, the old woman continues to stand guard. Inside, Ted sets up his next shot.

Dite is seated on the floor.

Ted walks towards the door and turns the key. The old woman's ears catch the sound of the door locking and glances over.

The set is almost ready. A cardboard chariot is in place. Ted brings out a huge jaguar prop and places it in front of the chariot.

"Do you need any help?" Dite asks.

"Take off your top," Ted commands.

He struggles to carry out a dragon. It is as large as the jaguar. He attaches the long leather reigns to the two beasts. Dite, topless, struts over to the chariot. Her hair, as ordered, is in a bun. Ted places a crown upon her head.

"Do you want me to hold the reigns?"

"With your left hand."

He places a sword in her right hand.

"Hold this up—like this."

He straps her huge breasts into a metal breastplate. Four holes allow her breasts and two bulges of fat to protrude, threateningly. They are as menacing as the beasts before her.

He picks up his Zeiss. A turn of a switch casts a red light on her, bathing her in its blood-like hue. She smiles. In the light, her teeth appear brownish. Ted kneels before the beasts. They appear as if they are lunging forward, devouring those caught in their path. Dite raises the sword. Her mouth continues to open. The camera picks up the darkness within. Click. This time there is no flash.

Outside, in the heat, the old woman recites, half to herself and half to an Indian couple that has wandered off the reservation (or was it out of the casino?), a verse she had memorized long ago.

At the studio. The sun has passed beyond the highest point on its path and is now inching along its descent. The dark windows prevent any light from entering the studio. The fan has joined the air conditioner in the defense of Ted's space. Ted is sitting at his desk, working on his manuscript. The door clangs. He knows who it is.

"I finished the books you gave me," she says, locking the door behind her and walking around the counter. She seems oddly assure of herself. Why?

He places his manuscript away and stands up.

"I left home," she announces.

"What? When?" He is startled, and yet intrigued. He senses a deep stirring in his loins.

"This morning. I've got all my stuff in the car. I had a fight with my parents. They kinda threw me out. So I just left."

"Do you have any money?"

"A couple hundred dollars."

"Where are you gonna stay? Do you have any plans? That's not enough for an apartment."

"I don't know. Can I stay here?" she asks, looking around. "Until I get my shit together, I mean."

"At the studio? Don't you have any friends? Besides, this is where I stay."

"I thought you had a home, or something?"

"Mina. You and I. We're beginning to explore. I call it *mapping*. I'm your…"

"Guide. You said so yourself."

"Yes. Together, we're going to explore your inner terrain. Find your archetypes. And like I told you, there's a place within you, a secret cave, a temple, that only you can enter. I can take you there. But only you can…Look, if you move in with me, it'll be the end of the exploration."

"I don't understand."

"You will. But for right now, you need a place of your own."

"I don't have the money to rent a place. Even if I stay in a hotel…I'll be broke in a week. I gotta get a job. How about if I sleep in your van?"

"I know a landlord in town. She owes me a few favors. Let me see if I can get you a room for a while."

Southernlands

At the market.

"They saw them!" several children cried, pointing at the Mayan messengers from the coast.

Pushing through the gathered crowd, the priests arrived and attempted to lead the messengers back to the monastery. The excitement was so pitched that it was not until several warriors appeared that the usually civil and disciplined crowd returned to order, making way for the priests and the messengers.

Quetz, standing in the center of the school with several other novitiates, was heatedly involved in an argument over the interpretation of the eight omens that had mysteriously appeared. When the party of messengers and priests entered the courtyard, the group broke off their discussion and gathered around. Soon, several of the chief priests, grim faced as usual, joined them. The Mayan messengers were expressionless.

"Welcome, friends," one of the chief priests began. "You may speak. This is your house."

Quetz leaned forward, making sure that he wouldn't miss a word.

"Not long ago three floating mountains appeared," one of the shorter messengers uttered, his Nahuatl accent strained and thick. This was a great wonder to us."

"We have already heard that. In fact, our own spies have been watching these mountains for quite some time," the high priest interjected, impatiently.

"After a time, we approached the mountains. We found that there are many beings living there."

"What did they say?"

"They do not talk with the tongues of man."

"Did they communicate their intentions?" Quetz blurted out, gaining the ire of his elders and the respect of his fellow novitiates.

"They showed us that they want gold. We brought them what they wanted and then motioned for them to leave. But they would not. Instead, they made the heavens thunder. We were thrown to the ground and had to cover our ears. The earth shook underneath us. Smoke arose all around us. The earth exploded. Full of fright, we fled."

"This is a great and wondrous event."

"Yes. We are very puzzled by these strange events. We thought that our Lord Moctezuma will know what to do."

"We shall take you to him. You shall tell him all that you have told us."

❧   ❧   ❧

At the palace. As soon as Tez heard that his father had been arrested, he excused himself from his teachers and ran towards the palace. Word of his father's arrest was already spreading throughout the city. Although most people did not know him, a few, particularly the various *tonalpouhque*, or diviners, who lined the outer fringes of the market, trading their ability to foresee the future for either goods or coca beans, recognized him. He had not yet earned the rank of warrior. Thus, he was still the wizard's son and under his father's protection.

When they saw him, they broke out in laughter. One, a rather burly young diviner, stood in his way, demanding news. Grabbing his shoulder, and catching him off balance by pulling and then thrusting, Tez knocked him to the ground and then dashed on. Several of the diviners called after him, cursing him.

Trusting in both his sovereignty and his people, the Emperor had left the palace unguarded. No one ever dared enter unless they had a right to do so. Tez loitered about the entrance, wondering if he had the backbone. Priests and other dignitaries entered and left. No one noticed him. He followed several for a few paces, hoping to catch some news of his father.

Fear shot through him the moment he felt a hand on his shoulder. "Quetz!"

"I left the *calmecac* as soon as I could. How long have you been here?"

"Not long," he answered, knowing that his brother's concern was as intense as his own.

"Do you think we should try and find out what happened?" Tez asked, secretly wondering if he shouldn't have phrased the question, "do you think we should try to rescue him?"

"Let's go."

The interior of the palace was as terrifyingly dark as the exterior was austere. The sounds of their breathing echoed back from the mocking walls. With their hearts pounding, and their minds wanting to scream out in terror, they drug their heavy limbs along the cold stone floor. Each step of their bare feet sent a muffled thud down the corridor, announcing their presence, laughing at their feeble courage. Passageways opened before them, beckoning them on to awaiting fates. Their nostrils flared, attempting to sniff out the best path. Of their many senses, certainly their eyes now seemed the least trustworthy.

At the palace. The Emperor Moctezuma ordered the old wizard to stand at his side. Other wizards had also been arrested and were now in the room, which included several members of the royal family, rulers from other affiliated cities, leading warriors and high priests. In their midst stood the Mayan messengers.

"Our great lord Moctezuma. We thank you for giving us an audience."

"These are strange times. The Emperor welcomes you and asks that you take our greetings back to your people," Cauitluac, the Emperor's brother, said.

"Tell us what have you seen?" the high priest asked.

"Very well. Not long ago three mountains—strange floating islands—appeared on the water. At first, we were frightened. Thunder issued forth from them. Lightning struck the land. Our warriors paddled out, hoping to understand this marvel."

"Yes, yes. I know of the floating islands and of the gods' strange request for gold." Moctezuma said, impatiently.

"Did they ask for quetzal feathers?" the high priest inquired.

"They were only interested in gold."

"Did they identify themselves?" Moctezuma inquired.

"They do not speak with the tongues of men, and their appearance is unearthly."

"Describe them," Cuitluac ordered.

"They are terrible to behold. They look like fearsome grasshoppers. Their skin is covered with thick scales, much like that of lizards. Upon their heads they wear the moon. They have the faces of humans but the fangs of jaguars. Their hair is like a woman's. And each one has the tail of a scorpion. That is not the worst. There are also giants amongst them—beings with four legs—wondrous to behold. And when they speak the earth itself trembles."

"Do they have a leader?"

"We are not sure. One stands in the front and bellows. We gave them some gold and some women to eat. We had hoped that they would leave. But they have not. More we cannot say."

"How hungry are they?" Cuitlauc asked.

"They are as hungry as locusts. They eat gold as if it were amaranth."

"Why gold?" Cuahutemoc, the Emperor's cousin, mused. "Why not quetzal feathers? Or jade? Or even coca beans?"

"We do not know," the Mayan answered.

"Then let the wizards speak!" Moctezuma commanded.

Tez's father, who was the eldest, though perhaps not the most powerful, stepped forward, shaking his head. He looked astonishingly frail at that moment, yet all gazed at him with respect.

"We have nothing to say to these things."

"Nothing?" Moctezuma asked, indignantly. "Nothing at all? What good are wizards, any way? How have they ever served the common good of our people? As the Emperor, I order you, all of you *sons of the night*, to interpret both the meaning of the Locusts and the eight omens."

"We will neither interpret the significance of the Locusts nor explain the omens," the old wizard retorted, shedding his frailty and drawing himself up.

"I am ordering you to do so," Moctezuma said, standing up, his fury filling the entire hall, forcing the priests and warriors back, leaving the wizards exposed.

"If Moctezuma wishes to know, then we shall say this: a great mystery is about to be revealed to his people, his city and himself. He must wait and see. Then he shall understand and know all."

"Sons of the night, I order you to reveal what you know!"

In response to their unrelenting defiance, the Emperor grunted between clenched teeth, "Lock them up and keep them there until they reveal the secrets of this mystery!"

But when the warriors attempted to take hold of the wizards they suddenly vanished, and then, just as quickly, reappeared. Moctezuma's fury rose. Turning to one of his administrators, he ordered all the of wizards' male children to be arrested.

To one of his aids, the Emperor said, "If they still refuse to comply, hand their boys over to the priests."

Northernlands

At the park. The sun is setting. Ted's Ford van sits alone in the lot at Stagecoach City Regional Park. Early moonlight has not yet illuminated it. Not far away, gangs of young thugs patrol the streets. Ted and Mina are sitting on a blanket under a tree, close to an old stagecoach. Ted is wearing a tight white T-shirt and blue jeans. As usual, he is wearing black army boots. Mina's feet are strapped in sandals, as Ted prefers. Her hair is in a bun. The red dress Ted has selected for her teasingly reveals her cleavage. Mina listens with the enthusiasm of a young woman in her late teens as Ted strums one of his sentimental folksy guitar ballads. Her eyes move across the grass and to a small flower garden. A slight movement catches her attention, transfixing her. A hummingbird hovers above the flowers, sipping nectar and then darting between the petals. Ted does not notice as the bird dashes upwards.

Half way through his third song he places the guitar down and lunges at her, pinning her beneath him. She struggles, but to no avail. He gently pecks her on the cheek. She mumbles something. He rolls over, laughing, taking her with him. Entwined in each other's embrace, he bites into her neck, sucking. Blades of grass stick to their sweaty skin.

Lying on his back, with a dandelion stem in his mouth, and Mina's head on his chest, he gazes up at the moon and the mountains. Mina reaches slowly across his chest and touches his hand. Her fingers gently travel the length of his forearm, finally coming to rest on his biceps. He flexes for her, impressed by his own bulge. She stares at his arm, watching as his muscle inflates and then relaxes. Using both hands, she measures the size of his biceps. Ted smiles, looking past her, his bulge and at nothing in the distance.

🍁   🍁   🍁

At the park.

"Ted? How did you ever get to be so old?" she asks, teasing him.

"Old? What do you mean—*old*?" he asks, defensively.

"I mean...I like you, but...ah...How does it really feel?" Mina entreats, fearing that she may have said something terribly wrong. Ted senses something and becomes uneasy. His breathing becomes shallow. He feels as if an alien shadow had crept between them, tugging at the forgotten depths of their minds, gnawing at the base of their souls.

"It doesn't *feel* like anything," he says, attempting to dispel the strange dark sensation he feels creeping along his spine. "You *are* young, aren't you? Okay. You don't know how it feels. You're old, and you're you, all at the same time. You have some memories of when you were younger, and they're right there with you, but there's a lot that you can't remember, too—maybe that you don't want to remember. Anyway, it's all like a quilt, with part of it folded under. You look back and you can recall just about every year. You go over almost all of the milestones of your life. But you can't really connect them. You have to force them into a linear path. Memories of when you were ten and twenty run parallel. And then you ask yourself, how did you ever get to be so old?" he says, drawing her into his own laughter, finally forgetting his previous discomfort.

"Did you ever want to get old?" she asks, looking around at the unfamiliar trees and landscape, forcing him back to the topic.

"They say you don't have a choice, don't they?" His voice belies his growing irritation. "It's not like you can run away from it, is it?"

She turns around and rests her back against his chest. The back of her head is gently positioned on his shoulder. He hesitates before placing his hands on her hips.

"Do you ever think about death?" she whispers, her voice trembling slightly. Using both hands, she wraps his arms tightly around her waist as she waits for his reply.

*   *   *

At the studio. It is three o'clock in the morning. Getting out of the van, Ted and Mina walk silently towards the studio, their hands clasped together. The moment he unlocks the door the neon red sign above the store—*Studio Mictlan*—bathes them in a dull blood-like hue. Mina notices that the studio seems somehow different at night. She walks towards the wardrobe and undresses before the mirror. Ted watches, enjoying the fact that at the same moment he can see her from four sides. Naked, she turns and faces him, her backside reflecting in the mirror. Looking down at the bloodless hue of his skin, he wonders at the sun-ripened color of hers.

"Are you sure you're ready?" he asks, walking towards her.

She nods.

"It's over there," he says, pointing at another closet.

When she renters the room, she discovers that the scene is set. The CD-player is on. She hears the rhythmic sounds of waves crashing against the shore. A giant fiberglass rock sits in the middle of the set. She sits down upon the rock. The ocean is behind her. Her hair is in a bun. She has a crown upon her head. Her legs are tightly bound in a rubber mermaid outfit.

"You're so beautiful. Lift your legs a little—so that the flippers are off the sand," he commands.

She obliges, smiling. Zeiss in hand, he paces back and forth, looking for the right angle. The camera zooms in on her and then pulls back.

"What's wrong?" she asks, her voice rising.

"It's not right. I need you to dig inside of yourself. Go deep."

"I am," she says, her smile beginning to recede.

"You're not! Damn it! You think I can't see that! You think this is a game, don't you? I'm too old for games! Now dig or get out!"

"I can't," she cries. Her face becomes drawn, cracking her make-up.

His anger becomes threatening.

She attempts to stand and flee, but the rubber outfit prevents her from doing so. In her fear, she falls. A light flashes. Ted fires again. The camera clicks, catching her humiliation, her weakness, fear and flight.

Southernlands

At the palace. The old wizard faced the Emperor squarely. Neither disrespected the other. Both understood that the other was master of his sphere, however different those realms might be.

"If you do not comply with my wishes, I shall have both of your sons delivered to the priests," Moctezuma threatened. "And that goes for all the other wizards' children, too!"

"We have every intention of fulfilling your desires, my lord. However, when our mission has been completed, we ask that we be once again freed from your service, and that our sons be released."

"Agreed. Now, the Locust gods are still on the coast."

"So I have heard."

"As you know, there is great dissension amongst the wise as to their true identity. Being a man of learning, I have formed an opinion, which is based on my reading of the sacred *tonalpoualli.*"

"My lord. We are wizards. Divination is of only secondary interest to us. Fools seek to know in order to avoid fate—as if that were even possible!" the old wizard said, laughing and then spitting. The Emperor reigned in his anger.

"You wizards have always been a stiff necked and incorrigible lot. All right. Together with some of our priests…"

"Priests! Hah!" The old wizard spat again, challenging the Emperor with his eyes.

"Together with some priests, you are going to go to the coast and turn these Locust gods away. Blind them and then drive them back into the sea," Moctezuma ordered, looking tired beyond his years.

"I understand that you have already tried and failed."

The Emperor's head hung at the wizard's rebuke. "We have and it did."

"On several occasions, correct?"

"Yes."

"You've tried to beguile them with mirrors, I hear. You fools! Don't you know that when a Locust looks into a mirror it does not behold its own reflection? Are even the most elementary mysteries hidden from you?"

"Enough of your sarcasm. You are our last hope, old man."

"Until you have given up all hope," the old wizard concluded, leaving the deeply depressed Emperor to his dark thoughts of foreboding.

✿   ✿   ✿

At the palace. Cuitlahuac strode proudly, head held high, into his brother's chambers. He found the Emperor studying the divinatory calendar, surrounded by priests and diviners. Moctezuma did not look up.

"Are you absolutely certain?" the Emperor asked, his deep concern revealing itself in his voice.

"We are," the priests replied.

"Certain of what?" Cuitlahuac asked, a note of irony catching the last syllable.

"Your intrusions are most welcome, brother. However, I wish you would show our priests more respect."

"It is all right," the high priest said. His voice was unusually strong, considering that his body, crushed from the rigors of fasting and bleeding, appeared as little more than a skeleton.

"I understand your brother well, despite the fact that we are not like-minded in all things. We love him deeply and thank the gods daily that he's not emperor." All of the gathered priests' eyes danced with laughter.

Cuitlahuac returned the priest's humor with a gentle smile.

"I, too, am glad this burden has not fallen on my shoulders. Nevertheless, I fear for you, brother."

"Ah? So, even you are aware of the prophecies?" the high priest asked, with irony.

"If it is *Him*, than it shall be…"

"It can be no other than Him," Moctezuma interrupted. "The Sun is ending. He has arrived, as foretold."

"How can you be sure? They are debating this right now in Cholula, the very heart of learning," Cuitlahuac pondered, his voice cracking.

"And how are the Cholultecans leaning?" the Emperor inquired, his own mind already made up.

"Most of the learned believe that the Locusts have nothing to do with our Lord Quetzalcoatl."

"Ridiculous!" the high priest snorted.

"Alas, for how long have we lived in our own delusions?" Cuitlahuac questioned, his voice pleading. "We thought the Fifth Sun would never end. All these years, were we wrong? It seems that the Maya, the Toltecas, and the Teotihuacanos understood these matters better than we."

"He is right, brother. Already the plans have been drawn up. I am to depart tonight."

"What?"

"Yes. The throne rightfully belongs to our Lord Quetzalcoatl. I have only kept it safe for him, just as our fathers had. I am but the steward. He is the Emperor."

"Leave us!" Cuitlahuac ordered—the anger in his voice apparent. Quickly, the priests bowed and withdrew.

"My brother," he said, placing a gentle hand on the Emperor's shoulder, "you are being beguiled by fools. If they were wrong about the Sun, how can you fully trust them in this matter?"

"I know them. I, too, am a priest, am I not? I, too, have spent my life studying the mysteries, have I not? We are like-minded," the Emperor answered.

"Yes. But many things have been hidden from both men and gods. My brother, I implore you, do not vacate the throne until your emissary of wizards have completed their mission."

"I desire to call the mission off. We must accept our fate."

"Not until we are certain of what that fate might be. Or have you so easily discounted all of the other prophecies? How can you be certain that they are not the Monsters of the Twilight, rather than our beloved Lord?"

"The time is ripe. If He is to return, he must return in I-Reed."

"I do not deny that. But you mustn't call off the mission. You yourself have said that they are our only hope. And even now, as we speak, the Otomi are poised to strike."

"When?" the Emperor asked, surprised by the news. "Why wasn't I informed?"

"Today. I have placed spies in the region."

"What are their numbers?"

"The Locusts and the four legged gods number close to a thousand. The Otomi are like rocks on a hill. They shall prevail."

"We shall see. Indeed, we shall see."

Northernlands

At the studio. The sun is beginning to set. Ted has not seen Mina for several weeks. Except for an occasional visitor, usually a Hmong, few people have entered his studio. When she does, she finds him working on his manuscript.

"I was wondering what had happened to you," he says, locking his script away.

She stands in the doorway. She has not removed her glasses. He has not looked up at her.

"That's what happens."

"What do you mean?" she asks, perplexed by his statement.

"When you start to map, Mina…" he says walking towards her. "Most people are frightened by the terrain. Our whole damn society's designed to derail your fright—to produce diversions."

"I know."

He stares at her glasses, noticing his own reflection, and then removes them from her face.

"It looks good," he says, touching her skin.

"I had them taken down. It's still raw. But I think it won't show."

"I never let it show. Lighting. Make-up. You didn't need a dermatologist."

"I was just too—you know—I would feel more confident if my scars weren't as visible."

"You've…" He looks at her top.

"Besides, you said I could be a model."

"Not *could be*. You are a model, aren't you? Isn't that what your doing here?"

"I mean, like in fashion magazines and stuff," she says, walking towards the wardrobe.

"Anyone can be model. And any good photographer can hype you. But if you want to be a *higher model,* you have to know your terrain, your inner cave. Even…"

She picks out a costume and begins to take off her clothes. Ted watches, intrigued.

"Are you listening? I said, even the…"

Her clothes fall about her ankles. She pulls on the sandals and walks naked towards him.

"Stop!" he orders.

"What's wrong?"

"What did you do to your breasts?"

"I had them enlarged."

"Silicone? Jesus Christ! How the fuck did you afford it?"

"It doesn't matter. Okay. A friend. My sister. But I thought that's what you had wanted! For the mermaid scene?"

"What? Bigger tits? You think it's that easy. Jesus. Goddamn it!"

He walks towards her; his stride is menacing. Mina takes a step back. "I just did it to please you. I thought it'd help."

"Look!" He turns and catches his breath. Pivoting back, he says: "The tits are okay. I like them—a little too perfect now. But you look Like some Goddamn soft-porno bunny. That's not what I'm after, Mina. And you can't exchange the outer for the inner. I want to see depth."

Mina's mind signals flight.

"I need a few minutes to set up the shot. In the meantime, why don't you go find the mermaid costume. No." His voice is calming, even reassuring.

He stops and stares at her, his eyes moving slowly over her exposed body. She feels vulnerable.

"I've got another idea. I want you to put on a wedding dress."

"A wedding dress? Why? Have you decided to marry me?" she teases.

"Just do it. There's a plastic bouquet of flowers on the table, too. Take them when you're done."

When she emerges from the closet she finds that Ted has set up the beach scene.

"You look good in that white dress. I like the way it contrasts with your tanned skin. Do you *feel* like getting married?"

"I...Let me concentrate."

"What are you feeling?"

"I don't know. Love? Joy? Excitement? Maybe a little nervous?" she asks, seeking for what he's after.

"Yes. Bring them up inside of you." He grabs his camera and begins to fire.

"My *abuela* used to have a lot of funning sayings about marriage," she laughs.

She begins to dance, her feet turning in small circles. Smiling like a new bride, she holds the bouquet in her left hand.

"Grab the hem and raise the dress a little."

"Like this?"

"No, with both hands. Drop the flowers. I want to see your sandals. Good."

"Now…lie down on the sand. Good. Spread your arms and legs. Just like that. Put the flowers next to your head. Change the angle. Wait. I'll do it." Again, the camera clicks.

Ted walks over to a chest full of props. He pulls out a large fishing net. Returning to her, his stride full of purpose, he throws the net over her.

"Roll into it. Good. Tighter. Excellent. I want the rope to cut into your flesh. That's it. Now, push your head back. I want your hair to be as sandy as possible."

Her body is wrapped in the net. Her arms and legs are pinned against her sides.

"Not quite. What are you feeling?"

"I don't know…Fear?" she asks, her voice cracking.

"Yes. Partly. Of whom? What else?"

"I don't know."

"Of whom, damn it?" he yells.

"I don't know…"

"The groom, Goddamn it!" he yells.

He walks over and stands above her, camera aimed. Ted feints a swift kick to the stomach, stopping short as the toe of his boot touches her. In concert with him, she pretends that the wind has been knocked out of her. Her body moans. Her mind is blank.

The sound of the camera clicking penetrates her ears.

"Smile!" he commands. "That's it," he says, watching her face contort. Another kick. "That's it, Goddamn it!" Explosions of light bathe her.

Southernlands

At the palace. With deep rings under his eyes from days gone by without sleep, Moctezuma welcomed both his brother and cousin into his quarters.

"The Locusts are marching towards Cholula," Cauhutemoc, the Emperor's cousin, said, his voice matter of fact.

"What would our forefathers have done?" the Emperor asked, looking intently at both of them.

"Fight!" Cuitlahuac answered, resolutely.

"I agree," Cauhutemoc added, the muscles in his arms and neck bulging.

"Fight! How can we fight against the gods? Against our own God?"

"Cousin. How can you be so sure that the Locusts are of Quetzal-coatl? Where is the eagle? Where is the serpent?"

"They are gods!"

"Yes. That cannot be doubted. Only gods could have so easily defeated the powerful Otomi. Not one of them was killed. No one was even injured. But are they *our* gods?" Cuitlahuac pondered aloud.

"The Cholultecans have concluded that they are not of Quetzal-coatl!"

"Is that so?" Moctezuma asked, surprised. "The Cholultecans?"

Just then a servant walked in.

"My Lords. A wizard wishes to address you."

"Send him in," the Emperor ordered.

The old wizard entered, his face looking more haggard than ever.

"Release our sons," he requested. "We have fulfilled your commands."

"Release them?" Cuitlahuac asked. "Have you succeeded in driving the Locusts back into the sea? Have you blinded them? Have you removed their fangs and plucked their wings? What of their scorpion tails?"

"We…"

"Our spies tell us that even now they are nearing Cholula."

"We failed in our mission, my Lord. We had intended to do all that you proposed. Along the way we were confronted by a drunk. Several of your warriors attempted to push him off the road. But he withstood us, standing fast in our path. Then, we realized who he was: Tezcatlipoca! He laughed at us. He chided us. We begged him for help, but he refused."

"Did he say anything?" Moctezuma asked, sadly perplexed.

"He told us, mocking us, to turn around and look at our beloved city. We did. The city was aflame. There were dead bodies everywhere. All was engulfed in flames. Sulfur poured down from the sky and bellowed forth from the earth, flowing down our streets. No brick was left standing. We could not bear to continue looking. The sound of wailing reached us. We hurled ourselves upon the ground, covering our ears. We could not listen to the screams."

The three lords were speechless. Shock was evident on all of their faces. Moctezuma steadied himself on his brother's shoulder. Cauhutemoc sat down and hugged himself.

"My people!" the Emperor cried, "Oh, my people!"

"I have fulfilled your wishes. The gods are not with you. Return my sons."

Anger welled up inside of the Emperor. Pointing his hand at the old man, he said: "Because you have failed, your sons shall remain with me!"

The old wizard bowed and disappeared.

Northernlands

At the studio. It is late. Ted puts his manuscript away and straightens up before leaving. Taking his guitar by its neck, he walks out of the studio, locking the door behind him.

"Zenith. What are you still doing here?"

"Serving the Almighty, I am. Are you going home? Not many customers today?"

"Too hot for most people, I guess. Nah. I'm just goin' to the park. I wanna work on a new song I've been writing."

"For that lovely young girl, I bet."

"Why…" Ted stops mid-sentence, shaking his head.

"I just wanted to share a scripture with you before you go."

"Zenith. You know…"

"Revelation 21: 3-4. It's probably the two most important verses in the Scriptures."

"I really don't have time right now, Zenith. And you oughta be gettin' home. It's gettin' late. And you know how it's not safe around her—in the dark."

"It won't take long. And I've already found it."

CHAPTER 4

Northernlands

At home. There is no moon. Ted pulls into his driveway. He has not been home for several days. Or has it been several weeks? The van is having engine problems. From the sound, it could be the carburetor. Inside, the rooms are dimly lit. Ted sits in his van for a few moments, thinking about Mina. He steps out of the van and walks into the house.

Moku, his wife, hobbles over to him and, reaching only to his navel, throws her arms around him. He warmly returns her hug. Their son is in the living room playing a Nintendo game. The boy quickly greets him and then returns to the game.

"You hungry? Moku make you good meal," she says.

"No thanks. I already ate. But it's good to be home," he replies.

"Oh. Moku happy, too. How you job?"

"Good. Many new people."

"Oh. Good for you. You hungry? How about drink?"

"Coffee, please. Thanks. But I can make it."

"No. Moku make it. You sit. Relax."

Ted looks around at the familiar surroundings of his home. He is always impressed at how skillful she is at using her one hand.

"What have you been doing lately?" Ted asks.

"Moku start English class. One day Moku be citizen."

"Really?"

"Moku go church on Sunday. We sing many songs. Very nice. You come next time?"

"No. I can't. Maybe in the future. Moku? I have to discuss something important with you."

"Yes?"

"You know how much I care for you, don't you? And for the boy."

"Moku know."

"Moku. I think I'm going to take another wife."

"No! Moku no like second wife."

"Moku. You'll always be my number one wife."

"No! Moku no want second wife!"

"I know this must hurt, Moku. But it can't be helped."

"Moku no understand. America one wife. You throw Moku away. Moku no *throw away wife!*"

"No, Moku. You'll always be number one."

"You throw ball with she?"

"No. Only with you."

"Then she no wife. She girlfriend."

"That's right. You're number one. Always."

Moku stands up and walks over to the fridge, opening the door slowly, and takes out a jug of pineapple juice.

He puts some photos on the table. "This is her, Moku. Maybe you can become friends."

"She very pretty. She very young. Maybe Moku think you too old for she."

Southernlands

In the gardens. Atototl met Tez in the Emperor's gardens. As soon as they saw each other, they embraced. Walking silently among the hundreds of various flowers, vines and herbs, they gently held each other's hands, and were aware of each other's steps.

Atototl had arranged to meet him here. Sitting next to a pond, they listened to the sounds of water splashing against the rocks. Atototl placed her feet in the water. Her paddling matched and was subsumed by the waterfall's relentless splattering. Tez reached down into the pond. The water's temperature numbed his fingers. Both of them gazed off at the sky. In the background, coming from the Emperor's zoo, a jaguar's threatening roar could be heard above the gentle murmur of life.

Northernlands

At the park. It is early evening. Mina has agreed to meet him. She is surprised to see that he doesn't have his guitar. Approaching her, she notices that his long stride is full of urgency.

He attempts to kiss her. She turns away.

Their path takes them around the park. She is tense. They are not holding hands. A group of youths, gangbangers perhaps, are playing street basketball. Some other kids are sitting on the hoods of their cars, drinking beer.

"Mina. Look. Modeling is no game. It's serious. We're dealing with cosmic issues—with yourself. If you want to be my girl, fine. If you want to be my model, that's a whole different ball game."

"I want to model. But I don't understand…"

"Why I have to be so ruff? I'm sorry. I didn't mean to hurt you. Look…" he says, pulling up his shirt and turning towards her. "Go ahead. Punch me."

She looks down and keeps walking.

"It's about discovering, Mina," he pleads. "Modeling is just a means, a way, to transformation. And transformation can only come about through discovery. And sometimes that's painful."

"Aren't you afraid of them?" she asks, nodding at the gangsters.

"Why should I be?"

"Cause they're dangerous."

"I come here all the time. They don't understand me, so they can't hurt me. Besides, they wouldn't be caught dead in an old Ford van. And I don't carry any money on me."

"Oh. But that's not what's it's all about. You don't get robbed or something because—you deserve it, or something. It just happens. Wrong time, wrong place. My sister thinks it's fate."

A couple of the youths look at them. "*¿De dónde eres?*" one of the youths calls out to Mina. Ted and Mina lower their gaze, cautious not to make eye contact. The youths look through them.

"They make great subjects," he whispers.

"Subjects?" His statement surprises her. It even angers her.

"I've caught most of them. They're wonderful. Bandanas. Their uniforms. Colors. They've even come to my studio. I usually do them for free. Make them look like *real* gangsters. They love it. I've even got zoot-suits…So they can be real pachucos."

She stops and looks at him, puzzled. "Those *vatos*? Pachucos? No way. I've had enough of that shit! They're out there shooting at each other all the time. Who knows over what! How can you romanticize that crap?"

"I don't support anything. But you're not looking at them. They're in love with their images. Their reflections." They resume walking. "And it's all about language."

"Language?"

"Talking. They're using their persona to communicate.

"To who?"

"You mean, 'whom'?"

"Yeah. I mean, like—nobody's listening."

"I don't know about that."

"That's crazy."

"Mina. If you want to map, you've got to start listening and observing, without directly passing judgment. Alright, here's the final lesson for today. Okay: the physical world we've created is only a symbol, a personification, of the real world within us. Try to remember that. Hey? By the way, have you found a job yet?"

"No. This town's dead. And the landlady—what's her name?"

"Dite."

Distant gunshots, east of them, are heard. They cock their ears but continue on.

"She told me she wants some rent or else I have to leave. I don't have any money."

"I'll try and work something out with her. She still owes me a few favors."

"I really don't want to stay there any more. By the way, I followed you home the other day," she adds.

Ted stops, looks at her, and then turns away.

"I guess now I know why I can't stay there. Are you married?"

"Yes and no. It's complicated. Hey. Hold on!"

"What does that mean?"

"Let's sit down," he says, motioning to a bench.

"I don't want to sit," she answers, crossing her arms, beginning to wonder if he's just another sleazy old man.

Ted leans against a tree.

"I was doing a photo session of the Hmong New Year last November."

"The who?"

"The Hmong. Asian refugees—from Laos. You know, the people you sometimes see in my studio. She was there."

"She? Your wife?"

"The Hmong have a custom of throwing a ball back and forth as part of their courting ritual."

"I don't get it?"

"That's how they get to know each other, fall in love and eventually get married."

"By throwing a ball back and forth?"

"Every year I do a book on the Stage Coach Hmong community. All photos. She was alone. Nobody…"

"So you played catch with her?" He is struck by the riducle in her tone.

"This is serious. The Hmong suffered because of us. We used them and then fucked them. The CIA, you know. She stepped on one of our land mines. Lost her foot and most of her arm."

"So now you're fuckin' her? Is that it?"

"Fucking her? I married her. And I care about her, too."

"What does all that have to do with you?"

"Hey! I was in Nam!" he booms.

She looks at him incredulously.

"So? Like in *Apocalypse Now*? The photographer, right?" The irony in her voice is now undeniable.

He shakes his head, bewildered, sad and angry. "I lost a brother over there. A lot of brothers," he says, his voice trailing off.

She realizes his anguish, and, uncrossing her arms, reaches out towards him.

"I'm her husband. But in Hmong tradition only. I own her house. Visit her. Let her cook for me. Take the boy for a walk from time to time. That's it. I told her about you. About us."

"You told her about us?" She has difficulty believing him. "And she just accepted us? Just like that?"

"It's gonna be hard on her. The Hmong are polygamous by culture."

"Everyone, or just the men?"

He ignores her interruption. "When they came to the United States, we told them that they have to be monogamous in order to be granted residency. But here's the catch: we told the men that they could pick which wife they wanted to stay with. That's right. It wasn't even based on seniority. The choice was given to the men. Moku lost out. She's what the Hmong call a *throw away wife*."

"I see. So when can I meet her?" she asks, her voice, stance and face a mixture of suspicion, irony and empathy.

"If you need a place to stay, I guess you could stay there."

"That'd be too weird. I'd feel strange going out with you and also staying with your wife. Does she know that we—you know?"

He takes her hand and leads her back to the van. She does not resist. Opening the van's side door, he motions for her to get in. She does. He slips in behind her and closes the door.

Southernlands

Cholula. The army reached the edge of the great city. The Tlaxcaltecan warriors were at the head of the march. The Locust gods brought up the rear. The people of Cholula, the cultural capital of the world, were in awe and fear of the arrival of their archenemies with the strange new gods. The Tlaxcalan messengers approached and requested that the leaders of the city meet with them. They claimed that they were friendly and wished peace, an alliance.

Despite reservations, the leaders agreed to meet them in the courtyard of one of the palaces. Gathering gifts for the strangers and their ancient rivals, and ordering that food for a banquet be prepared, the Cholulan leaders left.

🍁   🍁   🍁

At the palace. When Cauhutemoc entered the Emperor's chambers, he found his cousin sitting in the dark, depressed.

"My lord?"

"You are covered with dust."

"The urgency of my message prevented me from bathing."

Moctezuma stirred, stood up, and walked towards his cousin.

"What news do you bring me?"

"Cholula has fallen. The great city is flowing with blood."

"How?" he commanded, taking a firm hold of Cauhutemoc's arm.

"Our brothers and sisters believed that Quetzalcoatl would save them. They thought he would release a great deluge and destroy the Tlaxcaltecan dogs and the Locusts."

"He abandoned *His* people?"

"The Locusts trapped the leaders within a courtyard and stung everyone to death. Then they flew into the city, killing everyone they found. The people were so despaired—because Quetzalcoatl had abandoned them—that many hurled themselves from the temple. Still, He did not intervene."

"Has word of this spread amongst our people?"

"Already, the first of the Cholultecan refugees are arriving. We must prepare for war. If you will not lead our warriors, Cuitlahuac and I shall do so."

Anger welled up within the Emperor. "Are you suggesting…?"

"No, my Lord. We are your subjects. You are our Emperor. However, it is my right to speak my mind. And I say *war!*"

"My cousin. Have you and my brother taken leave of your senses? This is not the season for fighting. Have they sent us ambassadors? Has the time for deliberations passed?"

"Listen to me, my Lord. Does a wasp warn before it stings? Does a jaguar give its prey time to flee? These Locusts do not deliberate. They went into Cholula and slew all they could find."

"We must negotiate with these gods and continue to hope that they are from Quetzalcoatl," the Emperor said, more to himself than to his cousin.

"The Cholulans had hoped in vain. These gods cannot be appeased. They destroy everything in their paths. No leaf is left uneaten. No gold can satisfy their hunger."

Turning his back on his cousin, Moctezuma ordered: "Cauhutemoc. The decision—the burden—remains mine. My trust remains with our priests, our traditions and our knowledge of the mysteries of the cosmos. Leave me."

Northernlands

At the studio. It is very dark. Ted locks the studio door as he exits into the night. Zenith is still standing guard.

"Did you ever get a chance to read Revelation 21:3 and 4?" she asks, taking out her Bible.

"Goodnight Zenith," he says, walking past her.

He jogs to his van. He notices a woman parked in front of his space, watching him. The mirrored sunglasses perched atop her head look familiar, as do her features, yet...She opens the door and approaches him.

"*Orale!*" she says and smiles.

He is intrigued. He continues to unlock the van's side door and place his guitar in the back.

"Can I help you? The studio's closed. I open early, before sunrise."

"I'm here to see you, not the studio."

"Oh?" he asks, wondering as she steps forward. Her green cat like eyes shine, reflecting the street lamps.

"I'm Mina's sister. Masha."

She extends her hand. He takes it.

Southernlands

Lakeside. The wind was blowing hard that day. There was dust in the air. The roads were completely empty. Everyone had been ordered to remain indoors. Slowly, the large procession of Tlaxcaltecans and Locusts neared the lakeside.

Moctezuma, together with Cauhutemoc and the kings of Texcoco, Tlatelolco and the other great cities of the empire, along with countless warriors and priests, met the party.

When the Tlaxcaltecans saw them they began shouting and dancing, vindicated. Their jubilation clearly communicated to the others that they felt their time of power was close at hand.

Moctezuma stood upon a platform in the middle of the road, proudly surrounded by his subordinates. The procession stopped. One of the Locusts, clearly their leader, together with a woman, who identified him as their captain, neared. Without hesitation, the Captain of the Locusts stepped onto the platform and faced the Emperor. His lizard skin absorbed the light and his scorpion's stinger hung at his side.

"For centuries our forefathers have been waiting for you," the Emperor began, taking a deep breath.

"We kept the world safe, waiting for your arrival. Now, you are welcome here. A palace has been prepared for you. We ask that you consider our home to be yours."

The Tlaxcaltecan warriors began to shout, raising their clubs into the air.

Taking out precious quetzal feathers, the Emperor placed them around the Captain's neck. The Captain of the Locusts removed a strange unearthly green jade necklace from a sack and placed it slowly around the Emperor's neck. The two smiled, looking into each other's eyes.

Reaching out with both hands, Moctezuma took hold of the Captain's shoulders. The Captain returned his embrace.

CHAPTER 5

Southernlands

On the island. Tez and Quetz had been ordered to accompany several of the Locusts on a tour of the city. At first they were frightened. They were amazed to realize that the strange beings hardly seemed much older than themselves. They took them to the floating gardens and showed them the new techniques that had been developed. The two brothers were perplexed when the Locusts showed little interest. Then they walked along the canals. Most of the people stopped and stared, amazed to see the creatures. The Locusts paid them little heed. Taking them to the top of the temple, the Locusts pointed, barked and hissed at the crowds below. The brothers were bewildered.

Fearing that their guests might be hungry, they hurried to the sister city Tlatelolco. When they saw the market, the Locusts flew into the crowd. Seeing their approach, people scattered. Children screamed. Some of the off duty warriors eyed them, wearily. They thumped past the food and ran to the goldsmiths. Their thick paws clumsily fingered the fine jewelry as their heavily shod limbs pawed at the ground, kicking dust into the air about them. Snarling at each other with lips drawn back, they revealed their fangs. One of the

Locusts even put the gold to his mouth and bit it, causing gasps amongst the frightened onlookers.

Many in the gathered crowd gaped and commented on their peculiar smell. Small children held their noses and ran. A merchant approached. He offered the Locusts some quetzal works. One of the Locusts pushed him aside, hurling him into the throng. Seeing the merchants' fears, some of the warriors started laughing. The two Locusts opened their mouths and howled.

Tez and Quetz motioned for them to follow. Before leaving, they removed from the inner folds of their lizard skin several strange otherworldly clear jade stones and exchanged them for gold. Everyone gawked at the aliens and their gems. Together with many of those closest, Tez examined one of the precious stones. Finding it oddly warm to the touch, he ran it across his teeth. Unlike any stone he had ever examined, the Locusts' gems pulled and tugged at the enamel of his teeth, instead of gliding as stone does.

The brothers led them back to Tenochtitlan. The entire way the two creatures kept fingering the gold and howling. The boys took them to see the Emperor's gardens. Entirely uninterested in the flowers and herbs, they marched through the botanical section nonchalantly, trampling fauna under their hooves. They took them to one of the lovely ponds, but the Locusts could not see its beauty. Instead, they farted loudly and urinated. Finally, they took their guests to the zoo. When they saw the many wild beasts the Emperor kept for his pleasure, the Locusts reacted strangely, the brothers noted. They froze, hissed, and raised their long stingers into the air. Tez and Quetz motioned for them to leave. They would not move. Like scorpions, they poised to strike. Dark venom dripped from their mouths. Even the jaguars took notice of them. Finally, they lowered their stingers and followed.

Northernlands

At the studio. Masha enters the studio and looks around, her eyes sweeping the set. Walking to the center of the room, she gazes at the photos of former clients adorning the walls.

"Can I look at the pictures you've done of her?" Masha asks.

"They're not ready, yet." Ted studies her.

Masha walks around the room and looks at the props, curiously examining each one.

Ted watches her and then picks up his guitar and begins strumming.

"I remember when she saw your studio and just walked off. She does that sometimes."

Ted begins beating out an old popular ballad.

"Hey, that's Springstean, isn't it? *Born in...*"

"Come on. Sing along."

"Na. I can't sing. Anyway, we were pretty worried about her when she left. It took us a long time to figure out where she had gone."

"What do you like to listen to?" he asks, changing rhythm.

She picks up an Olmec mask, and is intrigued by it as she flips it over, studying its craftsmanship.

"Do you know any Johnny Cash? *Do-do-do I fell into a bloody ring of fire...do-do-do...*By the way, do you pay her to model?" she asks, interrupting her singing.

"She's learning. She'll start making money down the road."

"Can I see some of your other works?"

"Some of what I've done is at the library. I don't keep much here. I've also got some of it up it up on the Net."

"At the library? Like what?"

"Anyway, I've also published a collection on the war."

"Afghanistan?"

"Vietnam. I was there back in '68, when things were really hot. And I also publish an annual work on the Hmong."

"The who?"

"So, what do you do?" he asks, putting down his guitar.

"Gardening. I'm into gardening. Work at a nursery. I'm also taking a few classes at a local community college. Nothing big. You know..."

"Oh yeah. Which one?"

"How about yourself. Have you ever gone to school?"

"UC Santa Cruz—way back when. Nice campus. So, do you have a major? Accounting, I bet."

"Biology. I'm into dissecting things," she shrugs. "Mina thinks it's sick—cuttin' up frogs and stuff. But I like to see what's goin' on inside."

"Oh? I'm kinda into cockroaches, myself. What do you plan to do with biology?"

"I don't know. Med school, maybe—if it's not too late." She puts down the mask.

"There's more in the closet," he says.

"So—where can I find my little sister?" she asks, firmly.

"She's staying at my house now. With my wife."

"Oh? Where's that?"

"Across from the Indian reservation. It's the 12th house from the corner, if you're coming from this way. It's on Reed Street."

"I see," she says, and then whispers something to herself. "Is she there right now?"

"Probably."

Masha walks out. Ted watches her leave, wondering about her short hair and penetrating green eyes.

❀   ❀   ❀

At the studio. It has been several days since anyone has entered the studio. Outside it is hot. Ted is working on his manuscript. The door clangs. He puts it down and looks up. Masha enters. She does not remove her sunglasses. She looks fierce. Her nostrils flare. Ted leans back.

"Hello," he says, locking away the manuscript.

"Mina tells me you're a writer," she says, watching him lock the upper drawer of his desk and carefully remove the key.

Ted doesn't answer.

Sweat glistens on her skin. Her shirt is wet with perspiration.

"Are you hot?" he asks, clearing his throat and turning the fan towards her.

"I'm used to it."

"There are some cold drinks in the Fridge."

"Thanks," she says, walking towards the refrigerator.

"So, don't you ever get tired of photographing those people?"

"The Hmong? No. I want to capture their culture before it's gone—before it's completely destroyed."

"I think I remember reading something about them in the paper. Aren't they all on welfare or something?"

"Did you know that they used to pick up our downed pilots? Rescued them. We recruited them and then just walked away in '75. They believed in us! Before we taught them how to use machine guns and hand grenades, they were just simple hill farmers."

"'75?" she asks, surprised. "I didn't realize it's been that long."

He ponders the implications of her statement and continues: "'75 is when we walked away. It's also when Charlie overran their lines and attacked—burned—their villages. Most of them died trying to cross the Mekong—trying to get to freedom."

The door clangs again. Light and heat burst into the dark cool room. Someone enters. Ted shields his eyes, trying to see who it is. Masha cocks an ear and then smiles. A woman. She is wearing shorts and sandals. Her hair is in a bun. Masha notices the sandals. Ted continues squinting, hoping that someone will close the door. He steps out of the light. The woman walks over to him and kisses him.

"Hey *ese. Q-vo?*" Mina says to her sister, pulling her left arm around Ted's waist.

"When did you start wearing sandals?" Masha asks, observing the change in her sister's choice of footwear.

Ted looks down at Masha's tennis shoes. He returns Mina's embrace and clears his throat.

"So. You were saying…"

Ted attempts to relocate his train of thought.

"The Mekong," she says, her mind somewhere else. The two women eye each other, exchanging information.

"The river. They drowned. Just like that. They were mountain people and couldn't swim. But that was after they had to come down Viet Kong booby trapped trails."

"Are you talking about the Hmong?" Mina asks.

"So, they all drowned?" Masha imagines the horror.

"Most of them. And we didn't do a fuckin' thing to help."

Masha walks to the closet.

"So, Mina. What were you wearing?" Masha asks.

She doesn't answer. Ted watches her ass. He enjoys the way her jeans hug her curves.

"What would you like to wear?" Mina asks, ironically, perhaps even a little challengingly.

Masha examines a costume and then replaces it onto the rack.

"So, what are you working on? A novel?" Masha asks.

"A movie," he says, stepping gently away from Mina's embrace. Masha watches the way their fingers touch for an instant before parting.

"A movie?"

He is struck by her tone, by her strength, perhaps even by her condemnation.

"Hey. Somebody ought to make a movie about the Hmong," Mina suggests, full of enthusiasm. Neither of them responds to her statement.

"What's it about?" Masha asks.

He unlocks the top drawer and takes out the script. "It's called, *A Plan for the Liberation of Heimat.*"

"A what?" Mina gasps, turning around and looking at him. "What kind of title is that?" she laughs.

"Yeah, I know. Don't worry, I'll think up something better. I got a couple of alternatives: *Rebuilding Heimat,* for example. What about *The Conquest of Heimat*? Or, how about *The Conquest of Paradise?*"

"You'd better do better than that. Nobody'll go see anything with one of those titles—unless it runs in one of those old one dollar theaters. Hey, anybody hungry? My treat." Masha asks, chuckling.

"I never go out during the day. Can't stand the sun."

Both of the women stare at him, wondering.

"So, I'll go get us something. Chinese or Mexican?" Masha asks.

"There's an Earthquake Tacos just down the street," Ted answers.

The two girls smile.

"I'll go with you," Mina says. "I don't mind the sun."

Waiting for them to return, Ted's mind runs wild. He races through his props, trying to find something suitable for Masha. He imagines her naked, and then envisions her in the various outfits he has. Nothing seems to be quite right. He finds a wig. But, he realizes, it won't fit. Something inside of him begins to tingle—a deep sensation. For a moment, he pictures both of them on one set. He swallows. His throat is dry.

They reenter the studio with several bags of food.

"We stopped at The Old San Andreas Fault Burgers instead. We thought you might prefer a cheeseburger and some fries," Masha smirks, handing him a brown grease stained bag.

He takes out his wallet, but she motions for him to put it away.

"Getting back to my movie. I really can't explain it," he says, forcing the conversation.

The two sisters stare at him, sucking the chocolate and strawberry shakes up through their straws.

"Isn't that what a script is all about?" Masha finally asks, almost too sarcastically.

"I've got to show it to you for you to understand."

The two women stop eating and peer at him. "So, where is Heimat, anyway? Or what is it?" Mina asks.

"It's a city—just over the hill. If you're interested, we could go there tonight. I'll take you around. Show you my film. How about it?"

❀   ❀   ❀

Heimat. Ted's van won't start.

"It's got to be the battery," he complains. "It's too goddamn hot to get anybody to give us a jump. I'll have to go home and get my other car."

After a quarter of an hour, Ted arrives in his old VW bug. Masha and Mina topple into the back of the bug. Moku, who has now joined them, and is wearing sandals, with her hair tied up in a bun, hoists herself into the front seat. Their son crawls in between them. Ted starts the engine. He adjusts the rear view mirror so that he can watch the two sisters.

"Maybe we take Seenot?" Moku asks, unable to pronounce the old woman's name.

"Who? That old witch?" Ted's mood darkens at the mention of his studio's unwanted guardian.

"Yes. Moku think we have room."

"How about it, Ted? There's room for one more," Masha teases. Mina smiles, her eyes dancing in the mirror. "Besides, we like *brujas*."

Ted looks over at the old gray woman standing like a statue and shifts into first gear, punching the accelerator. The air-cooled engine revs, lurching the bug forward.

Soon, they are driving down Rabben Street. Tumble weeds smack against the front of the bug. Stray dogs move off the road as they approach. Ted uses his high beams. Most of the streetlights have been shot out. They drive past an old stagecoach. Someone has lit the wooden wheels with small white Christmas lights. The city of Mt. Beauty appears.

Ted makes a left hand turn onto highway 9.

"OK. Now, I want you to become aware of your surroundings. Behind you there are mountains. They rise over 10,000 feet. There are all sorts of deer…"

"Bears, too!" the young boy adds, annoying Ted, but amusing the women.

"To your left is another mountain range." Ted continues, his voice full of concentration. There are some nice little towns up there. To your right is Los Angeles. That's where the sun sets. Over your left shoulder is Bad Palmen. That's where it rises. Stage Coach City is in the middle, almost under the noon day sun—just a little off center."

"Is that why you live here?" Mina teases, her breath tickling the hairs on Ted's neck.

"That's why I don't go out during the day. It's hotter than Death Valley."

"Hotter than hell?" Masha asks, laughing.

"So, what's so special about Heimat?" Mina questions, studying the landscape.

Ted refuses to answer. The question seems to irritate him. Moonlight illuminates the fields. A few cattle are grazing on the barren field. The road winds. The hill's sides have been cut. The bug crawls down the steep incline. Ted has shifted into a lower gear. The engine whines. Masha focuses on the exposed soil. Moku notices and says, "It like wound." Ted pulls over to the side.

"You can't see it now, but there's a huge natural lake down there."

"What's it called?" the young boy asks, straining his neck while unwrapping a Snicker's candy bar.

"It doesn't have a name. They won't admit that it exists."

"What do you mean?" Masha asks.

"They say it's just rain water that never evaporated. But it's huge. So, because it doesn't exist, they say the city needs another lake. That's why they're building it on the other side of the city. One of the biggest reservoirs in California."

"You mean they've got a lake and…?"

"That's right. I used to be able to stop my car here and enjoy the valley—watch the sun set—see the reflection on the water. That was when this was just a two lane road. But then they expanded it into a highway, piling up so much rock and soil that the valley and lake disappeared. I tried…"

"Why?" Mina asks.

"Can we get out and see the lake?" the boy asks.

"No!" Ted answers, putting the bug in gear and driving on.

"I asked them to at least build a view point. A place where you could just park and enjoy the sight. They looked at me as if I were crazy. That was it. Anyway, I think I'm the only one who ever stopped here."

"Is this where the movie starts?" Mina asks.

"Yes. With a view of the lake."

"By the way," Masha asks, "is there a river down there? Or something which feeds into it?"

"There is a small stream—somewhere down there. I don't know. I've never crossed it, at least not that I remember." Ted stares down at the lake, pondering the stream.

They come over a hill and the city of Heimat comes into view. Thousands of lights twinkle in the dark.

"Wow!" the young boy exclaims.

Ted slows down to let them appreciate the view.

They reach the bottom of the hill.

"Hillman Springs Road." Moku reads the sign.

"We're going to keep going straight. But Hillman Springs Road is interesting. I don't know how I'll bring it into my film, yet."

"Why? What's there?" Mina asks.

"Hillman Springs Road. It's all there: Golf courses, churches—even a casino. You name it."

"So, why doesn't your film play over there."

"Because that's not the center. We're still about five miles from town, and I'm looking for the center—the heart of the city. Now, what direction are we traveling?" he asks.

No one answers.

"Bad Palmen is back over there, right?" Mina asks.

"We're traveling on the north-south axis. On State Street. There are only two axes in town. State Street and Muerto Ave. Muerto moves in a straight line from east to west. Where they meet—that's the center."

Ted pulls over and motions for everyone to get out of the bug. He leads them to the corner.

"This is it!" he says, excited.

"This is it?" Masha asks, dumbfounded. "What's so special about this spot? Just a couple of shops…"

"This is the center! The holiest place on earth! It's where the two axes cross."

"But there's nothing here!" Mina responds, perplexed.

"Oh, there's plenty here. Just nothing really special. That's it. That's what makes it so fantastic. Just like the lake, the center has completely vanished. Not in real geometric space, but in their minds. Their paradigm doesn't allow them to see it."

"Their what?" Mina asks.

"Paradigm." Ted answers. "We—I mean Americans—don't believe in centers. In fact, our whole culture is based on warring against centers. But it's right here, waiting for us to pass away, for someone else to come along and rediscover it. Maybe it'll take a thousand years, but someone else will come along and release it."

Ted begins walking, taking hold of the boy's shoulder. The others follow single file. The sidewalks are narrow.

"Years ago, this area used to have huge sidewalks—and palm trees," he says over his shoulder so that the three women can hear him.

"It's all been narrowed. The palms were removed. Now you've got more lanes, more cars, and more smog. Nobody walks here anymore, not after they declared war on pedestrians."

They stop at the corner. The traffic is congested. Exhaust assaults their lungs.

"This whole area, within one square mile, is spatially holy. In a way, down deep inside, they know it. Look, within this space you've got a library and two schools—knowledge, a park—nature and beauty, a hospital—compassion, a theater—art, restaurants—communion, and more churches than you can count—hope, wonder…"

"It just looks like an ordinary town to me." Mina says, looking around.

"As far as I'm concerned, there's no other place in the world like it. After the lake, the film uses an aerial view of the two axes crossing each other."

"Is there a main character?" Mina asks. "How about…?"

"I'm looking for somebody in his late forties to mid-fifties."

"Someone like you?" Masha teases. "Is he dashing?"

He ignores the remark. They enter the park and sit down. It is empty.

"I want an ice cream!" the young boy demands, looking at the freeze across the street.

Ted looks back at the center and then across at the hills.

"We see him coming over the hill. It's foggy. He's in an expensive car."

"A Jaguar?" Masha asks.

"A Rolls," he answers. "He drives to the center, parks next to the palm tree over there and gets out. He paces back and forth, listening. Something stirs within him. He feels it speaking to him."

"And then?" Masha asks.

"He plants his flag, you might say. He rents an office right on the center and starts to fight for his vision. He's got the only Rolls in town, so he attracts attention."

"Is he rich?" Mina asks.

"No. But he pretends to be. Appearance counts for more than reality. So, at first, they believe in him."

"Who're they?" Masha asks.

Moku takes her son by the hand and walks towards the ice cream parlor. Masha and Mina continue listening, watching the two cross the street.

"The townsfolk. He's got just enough money to make some minor investments. So, at first, he opens a few things he thinks they'll like."

"Like what? Video arcade for the kids? A coffee shop for the…"

"Exactly," he responds, cutting Masha short. "His various small businesses do pretty well. He even becomes a respected member of the Chamber and other local clubs. But those aren't his plans. But he needs a major cash cow. So he raises money for a small amusement park—a kind of year round carnival. Everyone loves the idea. A lot of people invest in it. He promises that the take will go back into the town."

"So, they put up their money for it, get to enjoy it, and then the profits go back to them?" Mina asks, considering the idea.

"Yes. No one's getting rich. The park provides jobs and the capital just circulates."

"Sounds like a pyramid scheme," Masha says.

"So, like that's it?" Mina asks. "Isn't there supposed to be like an antagonist or something? You know, a bad guy."

"Well, yes. Things start to go wrong. First, he meets a woman…"

"Why does it always have to be a woman…?" Masha complains.

"She's a lawyer, if that helps." Ted replies, laughing. "Besides, he's attracted to her—and that's always dangerous. Anyway, she doesn't trust him. She feels that there's something wrong. She makes a few phone calls. She becomes intrigued, and even worried, when nobody's ever heard of him before."

"Do they eventually fall in love?" Mina asks.

"I'm not sure, yet. Next, he formulates clear plans for where the two axes cross. He wants a raised circle, with a giant fountain, and statues…"

"Flowers?" Mina asks.

"Flowers, too. He makes an enemy out of a local commission. They start plotting against him. They even get the IRS involved. By the end of the year he's due to be audited."

"How are his books?"

"We don't know. The IRS starts to bug him, but they're just background tension. Storm clouds."

"Is everyone still going to the amusement park?"

"Oh, they never stop going there—no matter how much they start to dislike him. But the park starts running a deficit. Loans come due. They need to attract outsiders. They have to expand, secure more loans, you know. Pretty soon, if the park stops expanding, the whole thing'll collapse."

"Is that when they turn against him?" Mina asks.

"No. They can understand that. Meanwhile, their carnival has become sacred to them. Even local banks are willing to invest in it. But everyone wants him out. When they really turn against him is when he starts funneling funds to the center."

"Like what?"

"He buys up some of the buildings and converts them into art galleries, coffee houses, book stores, tobacco shops, and even a chess club. He brings in outside artists and musicians, foreigners, L.A. types, gays and lesbians, Afrocentrists, New Agers, Chicano militants—you name it. They become registered voters. It becomes a real bohemian place. He tries to get his people to push the circle through. He even wants to detour traffic around what has now become, in his mind, a plaza. His artists do renditions of how it should look."

"So, why are they all against it?" Mina asks. "It sounds good to me."

"I don't like it," Masha says, and gets up and walks towards the freeze. Ted and Mina follow.

"Maybe you should have him get killed at the end?" Mina suggests. "Gunned down—right in the center. Or, maybe he should survive the assassination attempt and bring in some old time gangsters...From Chicago."

"I was going to have it end with the lawyer discovering he's a fraud. He takes everyone's money and runs, leaving the town broke."

"They don't fall in love at the end?" she asks, stopping. "Maybe she oughta join him in New Mexico. Or, how about Old Mexico? They could be on the run together," Mina adds, squeezing his hand and giving him a quick peck on the check.

CHAPTER 6

Northernlands

At the studio. It is early morning. Ted spent the night in his van. He awakes, unzips his sleeping bag, opens the side door and steps out into the parking lot. The sun has not risen, yet. The sky has taken on a strange hue. Ted attempts to rub the sleep from his eyes. Zenith has already arrived and is waiting for him. His mind is still numb. As usual, he cannot recall his dreams. He walks towards her.

"Good morning, Ted," she says, cheerfully.

He does not answer. He wonders how anyone who is as convinced of the world's eminent demise as she is can be so cheerful at 5:00 A.M.?

"Did you ever get a chance to read that scripture I'd suggested?" Her voice is trembling with rapture.

"Which one was that?" he asks, yawning and fumbling through his jeans for his keys.

"Revelation 21: 3-4! Silly you. I have a new one for you! Isaiah 11: 6–9! You've got to read it!" Ted glances over at her for a moment. Her eyes appear feverish in the dawn.

He opens the door, slips into the studio and locks it behind him. The old woman laughs, pressing her face against the dark glass, trying to peer through.

Ted runs to the coffee maker.

"Isaiah 11: 6–9!" she shouts. The glass muffles her voice. Her breath fogs the window. The coffee machine gurgles deeply. The sun begins to rise.

❧   ❧   ❧

At the studio.

"So, your sister didn't like my movie?" Ted asks Mina, watching Masha as she looks through the Fridge in search of something to drink.

Mina is sitting next to Ted. She has her hand on his right knee. Her mane is thrown back. Ted's arm is draped over her shoulder.

"Not really. Did you like it, Mina?"

"I thought it was great," she says. "I could picture it. But what's the main character like? Is he likable or scum?"

"I picture him more as an adventurer of sorts. He's strong. Clever. Highly manipulative…"

"What I don't like about it…" Masha begins, opening a can of soda, "is that it's too much like your photos, except for your Hmong stuff."

Ted sits up, removing his arm from around Mina's shoulders. Masha walks towards them and sits down on the floor across from them. She takes a long gulp and then continues: "I mean, I like your Hmong photos. They're natural. They're not posing. They're just being Hmong, doing whatever they do. But what I've seen of your other stuff—it's too you."

"Well…" He wants to object, but she silences him with a wave of her hand.

"Take the fat bitch…"

"Dite."

"Yeah. That's not how Dite is! I've met her. That's not her at all. That's some weird fantasy you have."

"How do you know that's not Dite?" he asks. "Do you think that the Dite you see back at the apartment, the Dite that's obese, that's depressed, has curlers in her hair, and uses too much cheap perfume is the *real* Dite?"

"It's the Dite I see. The one she shows us. And that's the one I'd like to see. Maybe in black and white. Depressed and despaired. Not in a chariot being pulled by jaguars and snakes, fake boobs hangin' out."

"A dragon," he corrects her.

"And Mina's photos…"

"Hey, hey, hey!" Mina interrupts. "That's my business, not yours, sister. I don't need…"

Ted stops Mina from exploding. "So, what else don't you like?" he asks, attempting to hide his growing petulance.

"Your war photos. 'Copters at sunset. Tanks looking like giant insects. Fire. It's all way too romantic. War is brutal. And it's boring, right. I mean, you were there, weren't you? Why give it this aesthetic look, cleaning it up for tourists?"

"I think your wrong," Mina interjects. "Ted's photos snatch the essence of things. He's exploring the inner and trying to reveal it in his work."

"I call it mapping the inner terrain," he adds.

"I don't know," Masha counters. "I'd prefer to see people, you know, doing normal everyday things."

Ted shakes his head.

"Things like, I don't know—but the main thing is that you should show them in black and white."

"Why?" Mina asks suddenly, interested in her sister's statement.

"Because then you can emphasize the magic of space, lines, and forms. What I like about photography is that you catch the moment. And it's in that moment that you reveal someone as they exist in space, and maybe even the void—but not in your imagination."

"Where did you get all this?" Mina asks, perplexed by her sister's opinions.

Masha ignores her and continues: "It's like I'd rather see a photo of a cat hunting a mouse, or relaxing, or playing, or sitting on a roof watching leaves fall for hours, than I'd want to look at one all dressed up in a costume, looking like an Elizabethan lady or something. I think those photos are so stupid and demeaning to cats."

"I agree," Ted says, surprising Masha. "But there's a big difference between a cat and a human."

"Oh?" Masha asks, tossing her empty soda into a waste paper basket across the room.

"There's nothing more authentic than a cat, except for maybe a dolphin. They're there. They're in touch with their inner world. As an artist you want to encounter a cat just as he, or she, is."

Mina turns and stares at him. "So, why not a human?" she asks.

"Because the only thing authentic about a human is at the archetypal level. Everything else is just bullshit," he answers, resolutely. "100% bullshit. Smoke and mirrors. Constructed personas. That's who we are."

Masha considers his statement and then stands up. She crosses the room and peers for what seems like hours through the shades. Turning slowly, she stares at her younger sister and this new strange man in their life and then whispers: "We were there once, weren't we?"

Mina and Ted stare back at her. A cold chill permeates the room. It is almost as if the air conditioner had finally succeeded in its ceaseless vigil against the sun.

Mina stands up and walks to the window, joining her sister. Their hands touch. Mina notices the goose bumps on her sister's arms. They look at each other.

Southernlands

In the gardens. The lush vegetation surrounded them, shielding them from any other visitors. The Emperor had refused to close the gardens. Instead, he wanted the public to continue moving about freely, just as they had done before the strangers had appeared.

The great excitement over their arrival had slowly ebbed. Most people were attempting to return to the normal routines of their lives. A few, mainly children and the elderly, spent their time trying to catch glimpses of the Locust gods. Very few others had the time. At the highest levels of government in the land, heated discussions, even leading to angry disputes, were taking place.

Moctezuma had called a meeting. He loved his gardens, and felt that it was only here, surrounded by beauty, that one could discover the Way.

"Are these beings emissaries of Quetzalcoatl?" Moctezuma asked, looking intently from face to face.

"They are, my lord," the high priest answered. "The *tonalpoualli* confirms it without doubt."

"I disagree!" Cauhtemoc answered, assertively.

Everyone turned towards him.

"I've uttered it before, and I'll proclaim it again. The Locusts have nothing to do with Quetzalcoatl." He turned to the high priest, who was expressionless and serene. "They showed no interest in quetzal and they are only hungry for gold. What is gold to Quetzalcoatl?"

"And they massacred everyone in Cholula," the Emperor's brother, Cuitlauc, said—almost to himself. And then speaking up, he added, "And we found some islanders. They were lost at sea. They told us to beware. They said the Locust gods are insatiable. After they ate their gold, and all the plants, they feasted on their women and children. Everything. The great islands are dead."

"That explains why trade has stopped," Moctezuma pondered.

"None of this proves that they are not from Quetzalcoatl," the high priest challenged. "Who knows in what manner our Lord would return."

"Quetzalcoatl? Voracious? I hardly believe it," the Emperor's brother gasped.

"Nor I," Cauhtemoc added. "Is he not the most gentle of gods?"

"Of course. But roused to anger?"

"Yes," Moctezuma interrupted. "He is the founder of civilization itself. But creation is impossible without destruction. He comes to initiate us into a new age. New mysteries. New truths. New Knowledge. Thus, he must first burn away the old."

Moctezuma and Cuitlauc's eyes met and held each other. Dread danced between them, whispering to each of them. Neither looked away. Finally, the old wizard who had stood silent for so long spoke up.

"I was there when Tezcatlipoca showed us a vision of what is to be. Terrible. Our great city shall be lost. However, he never spoke of his brother our Lord. Surely, if these monsters were ambassadors of the Feathered Serpent, would not Tezcatlipoca have told us so?"

"Exactly!" Cauhtemoc shouted, raising his fist into the air. "We have been deceived. We must remove the scales from our eyes. Let us catch the Locusts and offer them to the gods. They love gold. I say we offer them to Xipe Totec. Let the priests flay them and dance in their lizard skins. Let Xipe Totec rejoice."

The old wizard steadied himself on his staff. "Do not become fools," he warned. "Does it really matter who they are?" He looked from face to face, shaming each of them. "Like cowards you desire to know. Like mice you run from the sun." He spat, a wad of spittle hitting the ground. His eyes locked on Moctezuma.

"Pain and terror. That is what has been allotted to mankind. There is nothing else. For one hundred and fifty years our forefathers crossed the desert. How many died in the heat, and the Sun, and for lack of water? Still, they accepted their fate. They knew that there was nothing else. In scorching temperatures our priests carried Huitzilopotzli on their backs. They listened and followed. They did not shirk, even when he brought them to this place of bitter waters, even when he gave them this cursed swampy island. No. They did not shirk from their fate. Now we must learn a new lesson. We must not only learn to accept our fate, as our forefathers in their humility did, but we, in our exaltation, the mightiest of all peoples, must learn to love our fate. This is the final great mystery Huitzilopotzli wishes us to learn. To love our fate, my lords, and nothing else."

Hearing the old wizard's words, the high priest shuddered. The three lords looked intently at each other and then looked away, wondering, contemplatively, how they would meet this new challenge.

Northernlands

At the studio. It is night. Ted has just finished a photo session with a young ten year old Hmong boy. Masha is sitting against the wall. She has been studying the entire session. The Hmong family pays and then leaves.

"I thought you don't do Hmong in costume?" she asks.

Ted takes the film down into the darkroom, which is located in the basement. While he is gone, Masha looks through the wardrobe at the various costumes.

"So, why'd you do that little Hmong boy like that? Like GI Joe or something?"

Ted walks to the door and locks it, reversing the sign so that it reads closed. Flipping a switch, the words *Studio Mictlan* appear above his shop, the image of the high-heeled shoe jutting downwards.

"I'd like to photograph you," he says. He expects to have startled her and looks for a blush, or perhaps a sign of refusal, or even anger. Instead, she stares back at him, a slight twinkle of laughter in her eyes. Ted notices the strain around the edge of her lips as she battles to suppress a smile.

"What would you like me to wear?" she asks, laughing.

Ted walks towards her, studying her.

"You have an interesting bone structure, and a nice figure."

"Nice?" she asks, teasing him.

"I don't know. We'll have to find out what your archetype is. But I'm not about to shoot you unless you're serious about mapping."

"I don't know if I'm serious about anything," she answers.

"We'll have to find a wig for you."

"Why? You don't like short hair?" she asks.

"It looks great on you. But the feminine archetype, the goddess that we're going to search for, has long hair."

"Ted. Fuck you!" she says.

He is taken aback.

"Okay. Wait. I'll try it. Go ahead. Put a wig on me." Her eyes travel to the floor and back, unsure of her decision.

He picks out a long blonde wig and places it on her.

"Now what?" she asks, faking a yawn. "Your archetype? It isn't based on a Barbie doll, is it?"

He studies her, ignoring her irony, and then places the wig's hair up in a bun.

"There's a scene I think you could do. It's powerful. Initiatory." He walks to the set and turns on the slide projector. The background goes white. He takes out a carousel of slides. Images of the ocean appear on the screen. The projector clicks. The surf crashes against the rocks. The water is tranquil. Now it is rough. The tide is out. Now it is in. The sky is blue and in the next photo it is dark. Clouds part. The sun breaks through. Heat rises from the projector.

"Isn't that up north?" she asks.

"Santa Cruz," he answers. He studies her expressions as she watches the slide show. He flips a switch on the boom box. Rhythmic sounds of the ocean, of the water crashing against the shore, reach her. A sea gull calls forth.

"Put this on," he commands, handing her a long sheer nightgown. She is surprised. She had not noticed that he had slipped behind her and had gone to the wardrobe. She is entranced.

"The changing room is over there," he says.

She steps a few feet away from him, and then lets her own clothes fall around her ankles. He studies her body. His eyes begin at her ankles and quickly move up her naked legs, buttocks, and back. He is shocked to see deep scars covering her back. She slips the sheer laced gown over her head, allowing it to fall gently over her body. Stepping swan-like from out of the clothes around her ankles, she raises first one foot and then the other.

Ted replaces the carousel of slides with a single photo of the ocean. The simulated ocean sounds continue. He carries a Styrofoam rock onto the platform and then strews sand about.

She walks onto the stage. The light illuminates her body. Ted steps away and looks at her. The forms and curves of her body are visible through the gown. He places a laurel wreath on her head. Kneeling down, he fits sandals onto her feet.

She sits down on the rock.

Ted takes up his Zeiss. She leans back and raises her arms playfully above her head. Ted stops. The camera drops to his waist, suspended by straps. He walks over and examines her.

"You…?"

"Yes?" she asks, smiling.

"You forgot to shave." His shock is evident by the look in his eyes. His face is slightly contorted.

"I don't have a beard, so why should I shave?" she asks, teasing him.

"No. I mean—you have hair under your arms," he stutters.

"That's right, Ted. And lots of it, too."

"I…I don't think we can"

"What's the matter, Teddy? I've got hair on my legs, too. Or, didn't you notice?" she asks, pulling the gown up to her knees.

"But a woman isn't…"

"Isn't what?" she asks, walking over to him and placing her hand on his chest, above the camera.

"Isn't supposed to grow hair?" Their eyes meet. Ted can't hold her gaze. He looks over her head and stares at the ocean, focusing on the surf and sky. She steps away from him.

"Poor Teddy," she teases. And then, quickly, reaches out and grabs his crotch, squeezing with all her might. Ted bends slightly over, attempting to move his pelvis out of reach. She laughs and walks back towards the closet.

Southernlands

In the palace. Moctezuma, Cuitlauc, and seven lords from seven surrounding cities were having dinner. Cauhtemoc, however, was not able to attend the feast. They sat around a large table. No one spoke. Over a hundred different dishes were brought out for them to taste. Still, no one spoke.

Half way through the meal five of the Locusts entered the banquet hall. Moctezuma greeted them and motioned that places be set. The lords looked at each other and continued eating, despite the stench coming from their guests.

Suddenly, the Captain of the Locusts jumped up and faced the Emperor, his scorpion's stinger raised threateningly. The other four Locusts followed, threatening the other lords. No one moved.

Moctezuma considered the situation. The Captain of the Locusts moved his stinger to the Emperor's throat. Moctezuma looked into his unearthly pale eyes. The Locust flicked his wrist. The Emperor felt a slight sting. Warm blood trickled down his neck.

One of the warriors entered the room. Spying what had just happened, he bolted back down the hallway. Within seconds he returned, and now the room was full of thirty, perhaps forty, warriors, each carrying clubs.

"Shall we kill them?" the commander of the warriors asked.

Moctezuma hesitated and then ordered, "Wait!"

Three of the Locusts moved between the Emperor and his war-riors, their stingers held high in the air, ready to strike. They hissed and curled their lips back, revealing their long fangs.

The warriors stepped forward, clubs held in striking positions.

"Wait!" the Emperor repeated.

"Give me the command, my lord," the first warrior implored.

"We can sound the alarm, my lord," one of the lords added, fear-ing that the Emperor was about to do something strange.

"Within minutes we could have ten thousand warriors out-side—each hurling stones and wielding clubs! Even with their sting-ers—even if they killed a thousand of our best—we'd overpower them. Sound the alarm, my lord," Cauhtemoc cried.

"Do not harm them," Moctezuma commanded.

The lords looked at him. Disbelief passed across their faces like a shadow.

"Tell the warriors not to harm them. I think they plan to take me captive, to take me back to the palace I have lent them."

"My lord!" one of the commanders cried.

"Tell the people and the other commanders that I am going freely. All this is by the will of the gods. Do not let anyone injure them."

Moctezuma stood up. The Locusts continued hissing. The Emperor crossed the room, walking in front of the Locusts. The war-riors parted, letting the Emperor pass. Two of the Locusts hissed at the seated lords, motioning with their stingers that they follow. No one disobeyed the will of the Emperor.

Northernlands

At the studio. The sun is above Stage Coach City. Ted is sitting at his desk. He has looked at his manuscript and returned it to its drawer. He cannot write. His guitar sits in its case. He would like to play, but cannot. The heat is unbearable. Water drips from the air conditioner. He walks over and turns the fan on, sitting down moments later between the fan and the air conditioner. It makes little impact. He walks to the sink, opens the tap, and fills a large jug with water. Taking it to the swamp cooler, he fills it and then switches it to high. The cooler hisses as it joins the other devices.

The door clangs. Someone enters. She locks the door behind her and turns the sign around.

"Oh? Am I closed?" he asks.

She smiles. Her body shines. It is bathed in sweat.

"I want to photograph you," she says.

He waves his hand, swatting at her words. "No one photographs me. I'm the man with the camera."

"I'm serious," she answers, moving towards his equipment.

"Don't be silly. I'm the photographer," he says again, holding his head as if it were too heavy for his neck.

"What's the matter?" she teases. "Are you afraid of the flash?"

"Masha," he says, reprimanding her. "Look…" In the unbearable heat he lacks the will to mount a strong opposition. His voice is tired, wishing she would just stop. "Be careful with that. It's fragile."

She takes the cover off the lens and pulls back the trigger. He stands up, takes a step, reaches over and takes the camera away from her.

"I told you, I stand behind the light. You stand in front of the light. That's the way it is. It's that simple."

"Who said, 'That's the way it has to be'?" she challenges him.

He cannot fight against her energy.

"What would you wear?" she asks, teasing him, trying to get him to wake up.

"Nothing."

"Nothing?" She laughs.

"I mean—I'm not going to wear a costume."

"Why not, Mr. archetypal photographer? Mr. explorer of the inner? Mr. surveyor of the soul?"

He turns away from her. Anger begins to well up inside of him.

"Come on, Ted. Let's find out what *your* hills look like. Or do you just?…"

"Okay," he says, angrily accepting her challenge.

"What do you want to see me in? A cowboy outfit? How about an Indian? Or an African? Should I be carrying a spear?" His voice reveals his petulance.

"How about…?" She looks around the room. "Would you really let me photograph you?" she asks.

"No!" he answers, sternly. But then reconsiders his remark. "No camera," he says, looking at her and realizing that the only chance he has of getting her to comply with his pursuits is to submit to hers.

"Okay. No camera. But will you let me lead?" she asks.

"It depends on what it is?"

"No. You have to trust me. You have to do what I tell you to do, wear what I tell you to wear. Do you think you can handle that?"

Ted looks around the studio and nods. The many photos, masks, props and costumes stare back at him.

CHAPTER 7

Southernlands

At the palace. The two brothers were extremely frustrated. Very few people at the palace had paid them any heed. On order of the Emperor, they were not allowed to leave. Quetz had taken to reciting poetry. He had even attempted to create a few.

The young Locusts they had guided through the city had withdrawn and shown little interest in meeting them. The two brothers had tried to explain the game of *patolli*, but with little success. At most, the Locusts had just mindlessly moved their pieces from square to square. Tez wondered at how little they were able to comprehend anything. Besides biting gold, and pawing at women, the Locust's were most amused by trying on each other's strange rock-like headdress, a game that seemed to never tire them.

Several weeks ago they had accompanied the Emperor and the Captain of the Locusts on a hunting expedition. They were amazed at how clumsy and noisy the Locusts were in their heavy lizard skin as they moved through the brush, frightening away everything within twice an arrow's shot. However, the great hoofed gods who carried the Locusts on their powerful backs were of a different nature.

When the hoofed gods appeared, with their flowing manes and tail, snorting fire, and moving through the throngs with grace, everyone froze and marveled. Unlike the Locusts, they were beings of great beauty, awe, and terror. The earth itself shook under them. They could dance upon the wind. Both of the young men had watched them in wonder, hoping to one day be allowed to touch their sleek skin and mane, perhaps to be granted permission to sit upon their backs, to outrun the wind itself, to dance in the light.

Tez walked to the window and listened, desiring to hear the hoofed gods call out. Quetz, too, admired the gods. He attempted to create a poem in their honor. Both of them were dumbfounded by why these great gods would allow the stenchous lizard-like Locusts to sit upon their backs.

❀ ❀ ❀

At the marketplace. The two brothers were surprised when the summons arrived, ordering them to the marketplace. As they pushed through the throng, Tez and Quetz caught sight of their mother and ran to her side. She looked tired. No one knew why the people of Tenochtitlan had been called to a general meeting, but speculation had spread like fire, buzzing about with the annoyance of a swarm of gnats.

The fact that the Emperor was conducting court from the Locusts' palace had startled most people. Initially, some had panicked. However, in time, confidence in Moctezuma and his knowledge of the cosmos had returned. Life continued on as it always had.

Rumor had it that one of the tax collectors and his sons had defeated a party of Locusts on the coast. In fact, some of the Locusts had even been killed in the fighting! However, most of the diviners cautioned against believing that sort of speculation. The Locusts were gods; they could not be killed.

Suddenly, silence, like a late afternoon shadow, crept through the crowd. The brothers strained their necks to see, rising on their tip-

toes. Every muscle in their bodies tightened in anticipation. Someone waved. It was Atototl. Slowly, she worked her way through the
crowd, slipping under shoulders and inching between waists until
she reached the boys. No one spoke.

For a brief moment, her supple body distracted Tez from the con-
cerns of this event. Quetz nudged him, commanding that they push
forward. Bodies became pliable, allowing them to pass. When they
finally reached a position where they could see, they realized why
everyone seemed shocked. Tez felt his brother's hand on his shoulder.

Moctezuma stood next to the Captain of the Locusts. His body
was bound in chains. His head hung to his collarbone. Gone was the
proud Emperor who had commanded the greatest empire ever. Tez
felt humiliated. Worst of all, Moctezuma showed no signs of resis-
tance. Why wasn't he fighting? Tez wanted to rush over and free him,
but he realized it would be futile. Besides, the leaders of the warriors
had been ordered not to resist the Locusts.

In the center of the square stood the tax collector and his sons.
They were bound to stakes. Arrows from all over the empire had
been bundled together and placed at their feet. The Captain of the
Locusts hissed at the crowd, raising his stinger. Black spittle spat
forth, burning the flesh of those closest. No one moved.

Lighting a firebrand, the Captain of the Locusts approached the
tax collector and his sons. The men focused on the Emperor, who
held their gazes with dignity, acknowledging them and strengthen-
ing them against their fate. The Locusts had forbidden the use of hal-
lucinogens.

Touching the torch to the arrows, the men were soon engulfed in
flames. Their skin slowly melted from their bodies. The smell of
burnt flesh filled the people's nostrils, choking their lungs, and stinging their eyes. "Why didn't they cry out?" Tez wondered. The pain
must have been unbearable. Everyone watched in silence. Then the
crowds dispersed.

Northernlands

In the van. Ted's back hurts. Mina has spent the night with him. She is still asleep. Her head rests on his chest. The sun has not risen, yet. Ted smells smoke and gently repositions Mina, attempting not to wake her.

He pulls on his jeans and then opens the van's door, sliding it slowly to the right. Stepping out, he realizes that the surrounding mountains are on fire. Red glowing lava-like lines of fire can be seen from where he is standing. Red and yellow Fire engines race past, howling. Forestry crews in their green trucks follow. Soon, prison inmates will appear—California chain gangs—wielding shovels and pickaxes.

Ted's eyes search the sky. There is no sign of any air support. By noon, though, water planes will arrive, joining the war on fire.

He can see the freeway at the foot of the mountains, running parallel to the old railroad tracks. Cars move at high speeds. No one stops. No one takes notice of the flames. By this afternoon, with temperatures rising into the hundreds, the fire will be raging out of control. Ted watches the spectacle and then, returning to the van, quickly falls asleep.

*   *   *

At the studio. It is noon. Despite the heat, Zenith is standing guard outside. The fire continues to rage. Mina is at work. She has gotten a job at a local fast food restaurant. Dite is at home, probably watching soap operas. Moku is studying English. Ted is pretending to work on his manuscript while he waits for Masha.

She had said that she would arrive by ten. Her tardiness infuriates him. Does she want to provoke him? He swallows his anger when she enters the studio.

He acts as if he hardly notices that she is late. Masha eyes him and smiles. Annoyance flickers around the edges of his lips. She is carrying a large package under her right arm and a smaller box under her left. He walks towards her. They look at each other. Neither speaks. She hands him the larger package. He holds it at a distance, staring at it. He does not open it. Since his youth, what seems now like an eternity ago, he has always been mistrustful of gifts. He can feel her will. Their eyes meet. He knows what he must do. He does it.

He takes out the pinstriped zoot suit and laughs. She smirks. Walking into the backroom, he places it on and then reenters the studio. She motions for him to sit down on the chair she has selected. He does. She reaches, teasingly, for the camera. He stiffens and she retreats. He relaxes. She opens the smaller package and takes out a hat. She places it on him, adjusting it at a slight angle. She places a pair of sunglasses, mirrored, on him.

She walks around him, observing him, pacing back and forth. He crosses and uncrosses his legs. She hands him a switchblade. He begins mechanically playing with it. The blade juts forth and then retreats, moving from and returning to its sheath with the speed of a hummingbird. She takes out an eyebrow liner and approaches him. Holding his cheeks with her left hand, she draws a thin mustache with her right. Although his body is tense, she feels his face submit to her will.

"The handsomest man in the universe!" she whispers in his ear.

Picking up a pad, she begins to draw. She stops. Ted hears something. She removes a cigar from its wrapper and places it in his mouth. He holds it between his lips for a few moments. She takes it from him and lights it, blowing smoke in his face. When she is done, he walks to the mirror and considers himself.

At the studio. It is night. Mina has joined them. No one speaks. There is a strange tension in the air that Ted cannot understand.

Mina is sitting on a chair in the center of the set. Masha is sitting on the small loveseat next to the window. Ted is at his desk. The silence seems to last for hours. He picks up his guitar, hoping to extinguish the void, and begins to pluck at the strings. An old Bob Dylan ballad rises into the air.

Mina joins Masha on the loveseat. They lean towards each other, their heads almost touching. Masha whispers something to her younger sister. Mina lays her head upon Masha's shoulder.

Ted looks up and wonders, but continues strumming. Mina sits up and shakes her head. Her mane whips about her ears. Masha watches her sister intently. Standing up suddenly and walking out of the studio, Mina slams the door behind her. Masha follows. Ted stares at the closed door.

At the park. Smoke from the fire darkens the stars. Ted and Mina watch the conflagration engulf the sky. Neither one of them has listened to the radio. Are the mountains being evacuated? Have looters begun plundering? Where is the wildlife fleeing? Ted looks at Mina. They embrace.

"I wanted to tell you something."

"I'm listening," he says, continuing to gaze at the red arrow like lines of fire.

She shakes her mane and looks away. "Are you gonna work with Masha?"

He smiles. "Are you jealous—of your sister? Come on," he says, reaching out and holding her face between his hands.

She pulls free. "That's not what I wanted to say."

"Well?" He becomes impatient.

"I'm pregnant," she whispers.

Ted's mind goes blank. Various possible courses of action flicker through his brain. He wants to discuss them with her, to use logic in this situation, to reason it out. Should they have the child? Should they keep it or give it up for adoption? Does he want a child? What about the fact that it is *his* child? But what about his art? Is it human or just a tissue? Could he really ask her to kill his child? Should he demand that she keep it?

She stares at him, puzzled. Her arms hang at her sides. She searches his eyes, but he seems to be looking past her.

"Just hold me," she says. He takes her in his arms and watches the fire.

🍁   🍁   🍁

At the studio. The old woman's gray hair is unusually unkempt this morning. Her eyes have taken on a feverish quality, expressing urgency.

"Did you get a chance to read those scriptures?" Zenith asks, smirking as he unlocks the door and slips inside.

He cannot work. He has lost all interest in his manuscript. He stares at his reflection in the mirror, out the window, at the clock, the walls, and waits. At noon, Masha enters the studio. She locks the door behind her.

"Put the zoot-suit on," she commands, her voice revealing her determination, her chin jutting forward.

He takes the suit and begins to walk towards the wardrobe.

"Stop!"

He turns and looks at her. She smiles.

"Right here."

He glances around, his eyes darting back and forth. But isn't that what he had always demanded of others? Had he not asked that he be allowed to participate in the ritual of changing, the secret of metamorphoses? But he cannot. He turns and continues walking away from her. When he looks back, he discovers that she is gone.

🍁   🍁   🍁

At the park. Ted and Mina are walking along a cleanly cemented path, which is lined by trees and grass. They are unconcerned with the tent city that has sprung up around them, families left homeless by the fire.

Ted takes her hand. Mina looks down at the grass, focusing on her steps. Sitting down under a tree, they watch as evacuees file past, moving like zombies towards makeshift showers and portable toilets. A few volunteer police stand guard, offering the families a token reassurance against the gangs.

"So, what are you gonna do? Have you thought about it?" Ted asks, pulling off her sandals and massaging her feet. His index fingers circle her ankles. His thumbs dig into her soles. She leans back.

"I don't know," she answers.

❦   ❦   ❦

At the studio. Ted has not seen Masha for several days. No one has entered his studio for some time. Outside, the fire continues to rage. Desert winds, an early sign of Santa Ana's arrival, assault the flames. There is no humidity. The sun is overhead. He turns up the air conditioner, fan, and swamp cooler. Suddenly, the power fails. He checks the fuses, cursing aloud. They are okay. He calls Dite, but she is not home. The door clangs. Masha enters. She is carrying a package.

Ted does not greet her. He is worried about the power outage. Masha sits down. Her body glistens, drenched in sweat. The temperature in the studio quickly rises. Beads of perspiration break across his forehead.

She opens one of the packages. Ted cannot see what is in it.

"Get dressed," she commands. He considers her. He senses that he dare not resist. If he does, he will lose her. Something tingles within him, daring him. He takes the suit from her and moves towards the wardrobe. He hesitates, waiting for her command. She doesn't speak. He is frozen.

She walks slowly towards him, studying him. Her ferocity is evident in her eyes. Her right hand lightly caresses the material of the zoot-suit; her left hand continues to hold the package. He can barely

CHAPTER 8

Southernlands

Tenochtitlan. Despite the presence of the Locusts and the hoofed gods, the city continued running in an orderly fashion. Of course, there were daily disputes in the marketplace amongst both the unlearned and the wise over the interpretation of the beings and their relation to the mysteries of the cosmos. Few people spoke in public about the burning of the tax collector and his sons. Within the upper circles, however, particularly the Emperor's brother and his companions, the fact that some of the Locusts had been killed did not escape their attention. Rumor, most of it untrustworthy, had it that they had actually bled, that under that thick lizard skin beat a heart. Some of the priests wondered whether the gods would accept Locust blood. Peasants reported having viewed the blood as being green and hideous. Warriors claimed that it was brownish red, and sweet to the tongue.

Northernlands

At the studio. Dite is seen walking towards the studio. Ted is alone. It is dark. The power has not yet returned. Outside it is hot. Fires continue to rage. Ranches have been engulfed. Horses have been turned loose in the hope that they might escape. Steers move along the highways, bellowing between fire engines. Planes drop tons of water and chemicals. Still, the fire consumes all in its path.

Ted sits alone in the dark studio. His eyes seem vacant. His lower lip trembles, as if he is caught in some internal conversation with an unseen spirit. The phone rings. He finally answers. Dite enters. Her hair is in a bun. She is wearing sandals. Ted looks at her, but takes no interest. She notices that he is paler than usual. His hands shake. He hangs up.

"What's wrong?" Dite asks.

"It's Moku," he answers, his voice seeming slurred.

Dite approaches, her sandals slapping the floor as she walks. She places a heavy hand on his shoulder. Ted takes hold of her swollen fingers. Mechanically, he touches her rings. His mind notes the way in which the puffed flesh curls over the gold and silver, absorbing them. His nostrils take in her one dollar imitation perfume.

"The neighbors found her in the back yard."

"What do you mean?" she asks.

"She hung herself. They found her hanging from the tree."

Southernlands

At the palace of the Locusts. Moctezuma stood at the window and considered his options. He was attempting to accept his fate. There was a reason why the Locusts, whoever they might truly be, had appeared. Who was he to oppose the mandates of cosmic law? From years of study, he recognized the fallibility of man to fully understand the cosmos—had not even the great elders of Cholula been mistaken? The divine plan often unfolded in ways that were only understandable in retrospect. Nevertheless, his duty, as Emperor, was to divine that purpose and submit his will. Yet, strange and mysterious forces—dark and dangerous—were clearly at work here.

Against his wishes, Cuitlauc, his beloved brother, was on the move, gathering a large pan-nation force to lay siege to the capital and destroy the Locusts. He feared for his brother. He had always been so brash, so stubborn, almost unconcerned with his cosmic duties. What fate awaited him should he dare to oppose the cosmos?

Messengers had secretly brought word that another swarm of Locusts, larger than the first, had appeared on the coast. They too offered jade. Yet, they indicated that they were at enmity with the Captain. The Captain himself appeared upset and had flown off with many of his Locusts and hoofed gods, intending to oppose them.

Nothing that he and his priests knew of had ever foretold this turn of events: two gods coming from the East, each opposing the other? Impossible! And what of Quetzalcoatl? Why would his house stand so divided? Certainly the entire universe had tilted off course.

He felt several soft hands on his back. He turned. A few of his concubines, their eyes gleaming, had entered his room. They took his hands and pulled him, giggling and laughing. He followed them to his bed.

At the temple. Women worked for months preparing for the festival. The god Huitzilopotli was adorned and beautiful. The warriors had all spent personal fortunes buying the very best featherwork. When the festival finally began, they would dance their utmost.

Tez and Quetz were both excited for the Fiesta. Despite their incarceration, they would be allowed to attend. Moreover, Tez had gotten word from his school master that he could join the procession. However, because he had never captured a warrior, he would have to dance at the back of the queue, the snake's tail.

The three girls, Atototl, Quiauhxochitl, and Matlalxochitl had come by and excitedly told them that they would serve as dance marshals. Everyone was looking forward to the Fiesta of Toxcatl.

Northernlands

In the van. Ted cannot sleep. Images of Moku hanging from the tree and of Masha back at his studio commingle in his mind. Mina has her arms around him, attempting to comfort him. He cannot understand why she did it. Wasn't she happy? Hadn't he done everything possible to provide for her? Certainly she and her people had suffered terribly, but—he tries to concentrate on the terrible tragedy—Masha continuously intrudes on his thoughts.

Ted places a hand upon Mina's stomach. The realization hits him. Fate has taken Moku from him, but life has blessed him with a new creation. A miracle. Scooting down, he places his ear on Mina's stomach and listens for...*Masha...Snake masks...Shed skin...*He shakes his head, attempting to free himself from her spell. He listens again, hoping that he might be able to hear something...kicking. Or is it still too early? She laughs and runs her fingers through his recently dyed jet-black hair.

"I have something for you," he says, with a note of melancholy in his voice. She looks at him and understands.

He hands her a gift-wrapped package. She slowly and meticulously unwraps it, careful not to tear the colorful paper. Opening the box, she finds an expensive pair of high-heeled stiletto shoes. Her fingers touch them, caressing their smooth texture and following their curves, the jutting knife-like sharpness of their point. She looks at him and wonders.

Southernlands

At the palace of the King. Tomorrow the Fiesta of Toxcatl will commence. The King of Toxcatl, anticipating the long awaited day, lay upon his bed, lost in his dreams. His chamber smelled of flowers. Hummingbirds flew in and out of the room, standing in space, fluttering their wings, observing him.

His four mistresses bathed his body with scented oil and fragrant kisses. Their tears washed over his skin, fortifying him for his journey.

In the past year he had grown fond of both his life and his concubines. How often had his hands and lips caressed their hips, thighs, and breasts? Yet he had always known the Fiesta would one day commence. He was prepared. It is what he had desired since childhood. Moreover, it was his fate.

At the plaza. Quetz took his seat in the section reserved for priests and watched the festivities. His mother sat down next to him, excited to see her son participate in the procession. Crowds thronged the palace.

Looking over, Quetz caught a glimpse of his father, the old wizard, looking haggard, older than his years, shadowed by the dwarf-like woman. A moment later his eyes scanned the crowd, but his father failed to be found.

Drums began to beat. Everyone stood up. The King of Toxcatl, dressed in the finest featherwork, and led by warriors and priests, entered the room. Hundreds of children pointed at him, screeching and squealing with delight. Everyone rejoiced. He walked with dignity and poise, flanked by his four beautiful maidens. Sitting down on his throne, he presided over the festivities.

The drumbeats continued, increasing in volume as the minutes wore on. The procession of dancers entered, jumping, kicking, twirling, and moving with grace and joy, flanked by women. Quetz spotted his three friends, wielding whips. He could hear their whips cracking over the drumbeats.

At the head of the procession were all the great heroes in the land, men who had captured many. They were followed by those who had captured less. They continued dancing, whirling and stomping. The crowd began to clap, keeping rhythm with the drumbeats.

Tez and those of his age brought up the rear. Quetz's mother screamed and pointed when she saw her son. Quetz leaned forward, happy for his brother.

The dancing continued and intensified. Hours that felt like minutes, aeons that passed in a dream, sped by. A few of the younger ones fell out of the row. Instantly, the maidens were upon them, whipping and dragging them either back in line or out of the ceremonial plaza. Tez, however, would not give up. He continued dancing, even when his bladder gave out, splashing warm liquid down his legs.

His individuation slowly ceased. The column moved as one, jumped as one, twirled as one, kicked as one. Was he moving quickly or slowly? Were the drumbeats sounds or hills that he climbed and descended? Did the maidens' whips cool him or burn him? Was there laughter in the pain? Was there ecstasy?

Something shook Quetz. Was it his mother? It seemed too forceful, didn't it? He felt a powerful grip upon his shoulder. A voice hissed in his ear. He strained to hear, and yet at the same time to ignore it, to wish it away, to struggle against it, to remain within the warm blanket of enchantment.

"We must leave. Now!" the old wizard commanded his son and wife.

Quetz looked at his father, not comprehending his urgency. Had the old man finally gone mad?

"Now! Before…" Quetz ignored him. He was an adult now, unbound to obey him. Besides, he had grown tired of his magic, of his disrespect for the ways. The old wizard reached over and tried to take hold of his wife's arm, but she too pulled away from him, frowning, and focused on her son.

The dancing continued, the intensity increasing. Mushrooms and peyote began to circulate. The audience jumped and danced to the rhythm of the beats. Where did the line between the dancers cease and the audience begin? Perhaps there was no line?

Quetz felt it before it actually happened. Out of the corners of his eyes he saw something moving onto the parameter of the plaza, encircling the participants. He attempted to ignore it. Someone pointed. His eyes followed the outstretched arm. The King of Toxcatl was standing now, looking concerned. His maidens looked frightened. A priest—one of Quetz's teachers, in fact—placed himself in front of the king, shielding him. More people began to point. Two Locusts approached the king, their stingers held in front of them. One of the Locusts lunged forward, his stinger piercing the priest, drawing blood from his ribs. Quetz's legs turned to stone. His eyes remained riveted on the king. Others began to notice. The king stood his ground. The other Locust rushed the king, bringing his stinger down upon his neck, severing it from its shoulders. Quetz watched in horror as the king's head fell to the floor, rolling a few feet before stopping, and his body collapsed, with its heart still pumping vigorously, blood spurting like a wicked artesian.

Suddenly, the Locusts rushed the dancers and the audience, stinging everyone at will. Panic broke out. Quetz grabbed his mother and attempted to flee. People shoved into them. His mother fell. Their hands parted, fingers touching for just a moment and then ripped away in a sea of screams. Warriors attempted to battle the Locusts with their bare hands. Bodies were cut in half. Blood splashed the walls and flowed onto the floor.

The crowd pushed against him from all directions. Quetz looked for the exits. People were screaming, running, moving. He hurled himself in a direction—any direction. A Locust, drenched in blood and ooze, rose out of the crowd, bodies piled up around him. Quetz attempted to push away from him. A wall of humans forced him on. With all his strength, he hurled his fist into the lizard-like skin. The Locust lost his footing and fell. Quetz sprang over him.

Another Locust appeared to his left. Quetz turned to his right. Something numbed his left arm. Looking down, he was shocked to discover that his arm was missing. He had been stung! Panic set in.

His eyes searched the floor. There it was! The crowd swept against him. His side was covered in blood. He dove to the floor. Bodies fell on top of him. Warm liquid bathed him. He crawled and groveled through the dismembered bodies, searching for his arm. He felt something cold and sharp pierce his side. Warmth gushed forth. Still he crawled, seeking his lost member. Then he saw it: the stinger—the sudden flash of light against…Darkness engulfed his vision. Sounds slowly faded, first muffled and then gone.

CHAPTER 9

Northernlands

In the van. Mina and Ted are resting. It is late. The van's curtains are drawn. The fire continues to burn out of control. The low-lying hills of Stagecoach City are now being threatened. Although the fire is miles away, the Old Pioneers Citizens' Corp has converged on the outdoor amphitheater. Bobcats, and men and women with shovels, are busy creating firebreaks around the shrine.

Ted is unusually melancholy today. Mina, too, shares his sadness.

"Why do you think she did it?" she asks.

Ted shrugs and stares at the van's ceiling. He wants to focus on Moku, but images of Masha continue to haunt him, gnawing at him, exciting him, causing his loins to jump.

"Was it because of me?"

Ted looks at her and rolls on his side, towards her. One palm braces his head; the other palm cups her left breast. He moves his hand up her neck and then rests it on her face, gently caressing her cheek.

"It had nothing to do with you," he says.

Southernlands

In the field. The high noon Sun blinded Tez the moment he awoke. Lying on his back, he had no idea where he was. His hands dug into the tilled soil, feeling its warmth. He felt another hand touch his forehead. He rolled over and found his father sitting next to him. Tez searched his father's face and eyes, looking for some sign that what he remembered had been an illusion.

"It's true," the old wizard said, looking up at the Sun, starring at it without blinking. Tez's heart stopped.

"Mother?"

"Dead."

"Quetz?"

"Cut in half."

"What about Atototl? Quiauhxochitl? And Matlalxochitl?"

"I'm not sure."

Shock followed by numbness froze Tez's soul.

"Are you sure that Quetz and mother…"

"Yes. My partner, too. Everyone. I was only able to save you."

Guilt raged through Tez at the thought of his own survival.

"The Locusts have committed a foul deed. All of the commanders, the great warriors, were killed, and all of the priests that were there, too. They have dared to trespass cosmic law."

Neither one of them spoke for some time. Tez rolled over onto his side.

"What about the king?"

"The King of Toxcatl was the first to be stung."

Tez closed his eyes. He attempted to suppress the horror of his experience, and to imagine the last moments of their lives before…

"What about the Emperor?" Tez finally asked.

"Moctezuma is still being held prisoner within the Locust's palace. He is doing his part. He has accepted his fate. What of you, my son? Are you prepared to accept yours?"

Terror shot through Tez, drying his mouth and throat.

"Well, my son? The next act begins."

"What is my fate, father?" Tez asked, his voice cracking.

"That you shall discover. However, for now, you must return to the city and join the siege."

"The siege?"

"The people have risen up. They have thrown off their yoke and are besieging the palace. The Locusts and the Emperor are huddled within. The Sun has passed the noonday point. The warriors have returned to the East. The Ciuateteo are accompanying Huitzilopotzli to the West. Thus, we begin our descent," the old man said, staring hard at the sun, his brow knit in pain.

"Your eyes are still weak, my son. Perhaps one day you shall be able to gaze, like an eagle, at the Sun without blinking. Do you see how it totters? Each day its wobble becomes more pronounced."

"Father..?" Tez began, his voice full of hesitation. However, when he looked over he discovered that the old wizard had vanished.

🍁   🍁   🍁

Outside the palace. When Tez entered the city he found it in a state he had never imagined. The once great orderly city was in chaos. People seemed to be running about without purpose. Second rank warriors struggled to gain control of the throng. The mob attacked the Locusts. The Locusts held their stronghold. Hundreds of people were stung to death in the fighting. A few Locusts were bruised in the battle. When the people saw them bleed, they hurled themselves at the gods without care for their own personal safety, throwing stones and yelling curses.

Tez entered one of the tents and found some of the warriors, many of whom he had known from school, at work making plans. They discussed the best manner of assaulting the enemies' fortifications. Someone mentioned the hidden passages within the palace that might allow for entrance. Everyone considered the possible stratagems one might use in a hand-to-hand confrontation with a

Locust. Warriors discussed known Locust ploys. An Otomi warrior, one of the few survivors from the great battle, demonstrated how one could rush in low under the arc of a Locust's stinger and sweep him off his feet. An old warrior asked whether or not the Emperor's rescue was of primary or secondary concern.

In the end, they decided that their first duty was to gain control over the rioters and to prevent any food or drink from entering the palace in the hope that they could procure a surrender.

"What if they threaten to kill Moctezuma if we don't back off?" an honored warrior asked, obviously concerned with the Emperor's fate.

"What if the Emperor himself demands that we cease hostilities?" an advisor questioned.

"What about Moctezuma's loyal supporters? What if they try and sneak food in?" everyone wondered.

A unified agreement was difficult to reach. The debates were heated. Several warriors left the conference, saying that they would have no part in opposing the will of the Emperor. In the end, however, most agreed that they would have to proceed, no matter how painful.

Outside the palace. Together with three other young warriors, Tez climbed over one of the ruptured walls and entered the outer zone of the palace. Twenty feet separated them from the two Locusts who were defending the narrow entrance. Tez, brandishing a club, moved in behind a huge Otomi warrior, easily twice his size, who had agreed to take the point. The third man in their party, bringing up the rear, had a bow and arrow.

The Locusts raised their stingers. The giant warrior picked up a large chunk of broken wall. Tez jumped to his right, attracting attention. For an instant, one of the Locust's eyes followed him. Grabbing a small rock and throwing it with all his force, he hit one of the

Locusts squarely above the knee. In that same instant the third warrior loosed his arrow. It missed. The giant hurled the heavy broken masonry. But the Locusts jumped aside. However, they were now off balance. Quickly, Tez closed the distance between them. His club came down upon the closest Locust's head, staggering him. Tez felt the clang as wood collided with the strange moon-like rocks they wore as headdress. The other Locust stepped towards him, and then lunged. His stinger stopped short as an arrow caught his shoulder. Tez wielded his club as he had been taught, driving the point into the Locust's reptilian stomach. The Locust fell, gasping for air. Instantly, the giant was upon the fallen enemy, grabbing him by the throat with all his might. Tez turned and faced the other Locust, who had pulled the arrow from out of his shoulder. The creature grinned, revealing his fangs, and then struck. Club met stinger. Tez felt his hands go numb as his club splintered. The Locust advanced. An arrow hit his hide and bounced off. Tez backed up. A third Locust entered the outer zone, charging the giant. It was too late. Tez picked up a rock and flung it with all his might. It hit the charging Locust squarely in the head, but he kept advancing. His stinger came down on the giant. A groan. Another arrow flew, hit its target, but again bounced off. Tez and the other surviving warrior retreated. From what they could tell, the Locust who had fallen under the giant would never rise again.

🍁   🍁   🍁

Outside the palace. No one had expected that the Captain of the Locusts would return as he did, with more Locusts, hoofed gods, Tlaxcaltecan warriors, and war dogs than before. But he did. Cutting a bloody path through their defenses, the Captain reentered the palace and sealed it from within.

Tez was surprised when—an hour or so later—the Emperor appeared, together with the Captain, on the roof of the temple. He requested that the siege be stopped and the market reopened. No one listened.

To everyone's surprise, the Emperor's brother, Cuitlauac, was released. Explaining to the suspicious defenders that the Locusts had charged him with restoring order, he let out a boisterous laugh. Gathering the surviving venerable warriors together, Cuitlauac called for a vote on the most important decision they had ever faced: whether or not to replace Moctezuma with himself as their leader?

Although fear and trembling shadowed their decision—a fear born out of a deep respect for cosmic order—most of the warriors reluctantly gave the Emperor's brother their vote of confidence. Cuitlauac quickly took charge. He organized the warriors into units. Ordering his men to cease attacking the palace straight out, he commanded that they form a strong line and starve them into submission.

When the Emperor's body was thrown over the walls, everyone was shocked and saddened, Cuitlauac most of all. They vowed revenge, promising to offer every Locust's dark heart to Huitzilopotzli.

Despite the siege, Cuitlauac ordered that the royal funeral be prepared.

✻   ✻   ✻

At the canals. At night, while the city slept, and Cuitlauac and the other royal leaders were in mourning, the Locusts attempted their escape. They loaded all the gold they could carry onto their backs and crept out of the city.

An owl, flying high above the city, spotted them at the canals and cried out. A woman, hearing the owl's screech, sounded the alarm, causing the warriors to race to the canals.

Tez jumped into a war canoe with several others and paddled with all his might. They caught the Locusts and the hoofed gods attempting to cross the canals. Working at a frenzy, the men drew up all of the bridges.

The warriors assaulted the Locusts. Hoping to escape with their booty, the Locusts jumped into the canals. The warriors followed.

Tez raced across the small land bridge and jumped into the water, swimming hard. As he neared one of the Locusts he dove underwater. Groping about in the dark until he finally, with most of his oxygen used up, and his lungs pounding—demanding that he breathe—found what felt like slimy wet lizard skin. The Locust dipped underwater as Tez pulled. The two wrestled. Tez released his foe and emerged, gulping air. A few seconds later the Locust emerged, slashing the air with a small stinger. Tez caught a sharp slice across the chin. Blood filled his mouth. He felt his lower lip swelling, and his face, from ear to ear, burning. Punching back, he hit the Locust in the neck. The creature gasped. Grabbing hold again, Tez pulled. Both went under—wrestling, clawing, biting. Tez felt the stinger cut his side. Attempting to grab it, he felt his arm go numb as it bit into the palm of his hand, and then ripped into his forearm. Despite the pain, he reached for the stinger again. The Locust wrenched it free. Tez's lungs ached. His head pounded. His mind shouted for him to surrender. The stinger bit him again and again. He felt his left thigh burning. Finally, his left hand found the locust's wrist as his other hand entwined itself deeper into the locust's long hair, pulling the beast's head back. Tightening his grip, his mind relaxed, knowing that he had stopped the stinger. Despite the continued pounding in his lungs, he held on to the Locust, making sure that they both stayed underwater. He felt the locust punching at his side with his other hand. He pulled his foe closer to him and struggled to remain conscious. With his supply of air exhausted, his teeth finally found the locust's throat. His last impression was that the locust had gone limp.

Northernlands

In the studio.

"So, what don't you like about my script?" Ted asks Masha, sitting in his chair and watching her shave the sides of her head.

"How does that look?"

"Sexy," he answers.

Walking over, and sitting down on his lap, she throws her arms around his neck. Gently, he touches the shaved parts of her head. He isn't sure how to touch her. He is used to women with long hair. Isn't longhair part of the feminine archetype? his mind shouts. She places both of her palms on his face and closes his eyes. An image appears—the jaguar: powerful, dangerous, fearsome, shorthaired, prowling. Another feline appears—the lioness. He opens his eyes and shutters. Masha laughs. Had she been reading his thoughts? he wonders. Taking his hand, she shows him how to touch her. He smiles, embarrassed.

Standing up, Masha walks over to the stereo and drops in a CD. The sounds of *Aztlan Underground* fill the room. She pulls up her shirt, revealing her stomach. He watches, fascinated, as she dances. She bends and twirls, teasing him first with her bosom and then her ass. He is delighted. Excitement builds within him. She kneels before him, pushing his legs apart. He anticipates. She springs up and dances away. He stands up and follows. Not having danced since his youth, he feels awkward. Her smile, the playfulness in her eyes, reassures him.

She takes his hand and leads him to the center of the studio. They embrace. His excitement overwhelms him. Taking her by the shoulders, he pushes her down onto the floor. She quickly rolls on top of him. Ted reaches for a switch. A red light comes on, bathing them in its hue. Their lips lock. Their hands explore each other: touching, fondling, caressing, squeezing. They cannot hear the music. Their minds are dark.

Somewhere within the hidden recesses of his mind, Ted realizes that the door has clanged open. But didn't they lock it? he wonders. Her lips hold his, sucking. Her teeth bite into him. He struggles to emerge from the depths, to open his eyes and look around. Her tongue flicks in and out of his mouth. He senses something and attempts to pull away, to rise to the surface of his consciousness. Her claws dig into him, holding him submerged.

Mina stands in the room, watching, horrified. *"Cabrones!"* she screams. Ted opens his eyes and pushes Masha away. Mina runs. She is wearing the high-heeled shoes he had given her. Her gait is unstable, tottering, as she balances her weight on the stilettos. Ted jumps up and rushes after her. Masha calls out, pleading with her sister to stop.

Her heel catches something. She falls hard. Instantly, Ted is at her side. Regrets. Pain. Sorrow. She rolls over, her stomach cramping. Ted looks from Mina to Masha. Something is terribly wrong. The pain intensifies. The moaning becomes louder. Masha spots the blood before Ted does.

"Mother of God! She's losing it!" Masha screams.

Ted looks down. He understands. Sadness fills him. He places his hand upon her stomach. He concentrates his will. He wants to stop it from happening. Mina screams. The pain! The life they had created has passed beyond them. Lost.

Masha is at her other side, holding her sister's hand. Her eyes travel the length of her sister's body. She sees the shoes. One heel is missing. They look at each other across Mina's contorted figure. Mina screams again. Her pain is unbearable. Masha pulls the other shoe from Mina's foot. Ted wonders. He cannot understand. She wields it like a knife. He attempts to block her thrust. He hears the thud before he feels it. His mind locates the spot—forehead, two inches above the right eye. Blood trickles down his temple. He struggles to comprehend. Again. This time the blow catches him in the chest, just above the heart. He backs away. *"¡Ya basta!"* Masha cries, embracing her sister. Mina reaches up and returns her sister's hug, sobbing. Ted looks around. He flees into the light of day, wondering why the word *valiant* flutters across his mind.

Outside, the sun has crossed its highest point and is now descending westward.

CHAPTER 10

❀

Northernlands

On the street. It is terrifyingly hot. Fires continue to rage in the mountains. Ted cannot find his sunglasses. The light and glare assaults his eyes. His head and chest ache from the sharp blows he received. Does he dare to go back for his glasses? Names flicker through his mind: Masha, Mina, Moku—all gone. Now only Dite remains. Or does she? Nothing comforts him. He is alone. Alienated. At least he has his camera. Can he leave without it? But his mind is no longer in control. Something within him compels him to flee. He cannot resist; he cannot go back, not even for his manuscript, camera, and guitar.

He has not gone far. The old white VW bug, always faithful, begins to sputter. Smoke belches out of the exhaust. He notices the red light. Oil? It is too late. A thud. The engine blows.

Ted leaves his bug on the side of the road and begins to trot. No. He is no longer jogging. His pace is that of a mad man. Sweat burns his eyes. His lungs gasp. His vision is but a blur. He does not wait for lights to turn green. The few cars that are on the road must stop for him. Tumble weeds crash against his legs. He does not notice them. Stray dogs see him but do not give chase.

Latinos, African-Americans, Hmong, and Laotions see him. Eyes follow him. His arms pump. His legs reach out before him, pulling at the terrain. He follows his body. He does not know where he is going.

Masha. Mina. Moku. He wants to run to Dite, to nestle his head between her large swollen breasts, to take in the safety of her apartment. His body runs past Dite's apartment complex. He turns the corner and crosses the street. The twelfth house from the corner, he reminds himself. Within seconds he is standing in front of the old chain-link gate.

Southernlands

At the canals. When Tez regained consciousness he found himself on the bank of the canals. Some villagers had rescued him, and a doctor was treating him. His wounds had already been wrapped. Looking around, he realized that there were others present. Villagers were still pulling warriors from out of the canals. The wounded were placed on the bank next to him. Dead Tlaxcalan and Locust bodies were heaped on piles and thrown into ditches. Later they will be taken to the marshes and dumped without ceremony. Dead Aztecs were placed on another pile. Sadness filled Tez's heart. How many of his friends—of his brothers—had died? he wondered.

A few, a very few, Locusts and Tlaxcalans had been captured. They were sitting off to the side, bound. Tez understood that they would soon be taken to the temple and offered to Huitzilopotzli.

He studied their faces from a distance. The Tlaxcalans appeared brave. Certainly, they had accepted their fate. But what of the Locusts? He wasn't sure. Their inhuman facial expressions were hard to read. Were they terrified of being sacrificed? If so, why? Didn't they realize that all of this had been foretold? Are we not only actors in a great drama, executing our parts? Tez wondered. Perhaps, he thought, they knew that Huitzilopotzli would not permit them to make the great journey?

Northernlands

At the house. Standing at the gate, Ted hears the sounds of rhythmic drumming coming from within the house. He hesitates before pushing open the gate and entering the yard.

A man, smoking a Camel cigarette, steps from out of the shadows. Ted stops. It is Moku's uncle, the undecorated and unrecognized veteran, the old soldier, the man who had fought and killed Viet Kong, who had crawled through the dense jungle looking for downed American pilots, who had gone down into tunnels, who had long ago surpassed his Green Beret and CIA instructors. Despite the old soldier's age, Ted does not want a physical confrontation.

"Hey Ted. You no come funeral," the old man says, spitting while adjusting his beret.

Ted extends a sweaty hand. His eyes focus on the glob of spit.

"You no beat drum for Moku. Why you no show sorrow? You sick?" The old soldier spits again.

Ted steps past him. He grabs Ted's shirtsleeve—gently, but with purpose. Ted stops, afraid. Despite his own service in Nam, he knows this man, this man with the pale watery brown eyes.

"You no lock up house when omen appear. What a matter? You no see? You no look for sign? You stupid, Ted? You no go see Shao? Fresno not far. Now what, Ted?" The old soldier spits again.

Ted steps past him. He walks to the back of the driveway. The old man follows. He flicks his half-smoked Camel to the ground and takes out the pack. Ted picks up a rust colored helmet and places it over his head. They watch each other. The old man pats the pack against the back of his hand. Ted sees the camel. The old warrior pulls a cigarette out of the pack with his lips. He does not light it. His tired eyes never stray. Ted buttons the chinstrap of his helmet and walks towards his Triumph.

Ponying over the saddle, he grabs the throttle and yanks it several times, flooding the carburetor with gas. Jumping up, using both his weight and strength, he thrusts the kick starter down. The Triumph turns over but does not start.

The old warrior takes out a book of matches and strikes a match against the box. Ted smells the stench of sulfur. The end of the cigarette begins to glow. Bluish smoke rises into the air. The old warrior walks over to him and extends a smoke. Ted looks at the package—at the camel. His hand reaches out. His fingers almost close on it. Their eyes meet. He withdraws his hand and returns it to the handlebars. "Now what, Ted?" the old soldier asks.

His left hand pulls the clutch. His right hand turns the throttle. He kicks with all his might. The four-stroke engine roars into being. The beast drowns out the drumbeats. Pushing the Triumph off its stand, he walks it to the street. He hears the old man laughing behind him. Something about the Shao reaches his ears. A warning? Tobacco smoke mixes with the Triumph's fumes. The two-wheeled monster roars again, pulling into the street, hurling off in a fury.

The old soldier flicks his half-smoked Camel to the ground and walks back into the house.

Southernlands

In Tenochtitlan. Tez entered the city and found people, thousands of people, busy restoring the destroyed palace and temple. He wanted to join the projects, but the wounds inflicted by the Locust's stinger prevented him from doing anything but nurse himself.

Within several weeks, Moctezuma's brother, along with his army, returned from Tlaxcala. Popular opinion maintained that the Locusts had been driven off and would never return. Well-ordered ceremonies followed. First, the great Emperor Moctezuma was properly buried. Then, obsequies for the many others were performed.

Hundreds of people were still unaccounted for. In fact, with the exception of his mother, Tez couldn't gather any information on the status of any of his relatives or friends. Both his brother and the three girls were simply listed as missing.

Calm began to return to the city. The new Emperor reopened the market at Tlatleloco. Lives returned to normal; trade began flowing; festivities returned; the great circular motion of the cosmos appeared to have been restored; and the Sun itself, always unstable and on the verge of tottering off course, seemed to have steadied.

When Tez reentered his school he was not surprised to find that the head schoolmaster was waiting for him. He thought that perhaps he was to be reprimanded. Had he not been absent for far too long? Walking briskly towards him, the master embraced him warmly and looked into his eyes. Then he understood. He had, in a sense, taken his first man—even if it were a Locust. He had finally become a warrior!

In Tenochtitlan. Resting on the floor of his parents' empty house, and aware of his aloneness, Tez thought of his mother and brother. Having dug through the many litered corpses, he had finally found his mother's body and buried her with full honors. His father had not appeared for some time. His brother's body was not to be found.

A knock at the door roused him from his stupor. He was surprised, and then overwhelmed with joy, to discover the three girls. The four immediately fell into each other's embrace before entering the house. Each had lost family and friends. Few had survived the massacre. Those few that had survived had done so by feigning death and hiding under the dead and fallen.

The four rejoiced—and cried.

At the Telpochcalli. Appointed as an instructor of the entering class of new cadets, Tez was busy at his new task of teaching them how to properly club an enemy when the high priest and the schoolmaster approached him.

He attempted not to notice the way they studied him. Inwardly, he smiled and admired his own confidence and new found skills. When the session was over, Tez dismissed his class and approached the two.

"Tez, I'm sure you know the high priest."

"Yes, my lord. How can I be of service to you?"

The high priest placed his old withered hand, with its long fingernails, on Tez's shoulder.

"I'm sorry about your brother, Tez. We all loved him very much. He would have made an excellent priest, one of the finest."

Tez acknowledged the high priest's condolences by looking away.

"Tez. You were at the Fiesta of Toxcatl. I do not need to tell you what happened."

"It was terrible," the schoolmaster interjected. "They attacked us without any honor—without even allowing us to arm ourselves—without even a warning!"

"Tez. You have been selected."

"My lords? What honor has befallen me?" Tez asked, drawing himself up.

"The Fiesta must be completed," the priest said, sternly. "The King of Toxcatl was killed—stung to death. You have been chosen as the new king. However, you shall not be granted the entire year. Nevertheless, you shall serve for a time. A season."

Tez did not know how to react to his appointment as King of Toxcatl. He felt dizzied by the prospect. But is that not what he had always longed for as a child? What every young boy had longed for? Would he not be doing his people, as well as the entire cosmos, a greater service than he could as an instructor? Nevertheless, he found his knees buckling, and had to mask his emotions.

Through a thick fog he heard the high priest add, "We've already spoken with your friends: Atototl, Quiauhxochitl, and Matlalxochitl. They have agreed to serve as your consorts. We are looking for a fourth woman now."

Borderlands

On the highway. The white Triumph 650 roars down the highway towards San Diego. Stagecoach City, Heimat and Temecula fall behind him. Fallbrook slips past without so much as a whimper of protest.

The Triumph cuts the wind like a spear, dancing in front of cars and trucks, out racing the clouds. Gas in Escondido? He pushes on. He cannot stop. What does the wind in his ears hiss? What secrets? What lies? Bugs assault his eyes. The sun's glare blinds him. The Triumph seems to guide itself. Is he only hanging on for the ride? He does not wonder. He rides with a fury, throttle wide open.

Quickly, he passes through Balboa Park, past the statute of the great Conquistador. Police see him but do not give chase. People turn and gape. The Triumph, with its stampede of unbridled horses, roars with delight, finally loosed upon the road.

Still, he refuses to ponder the pain he has left behind. Only the sound of the Triumph thundering and the wind hissing garners his attention, dreaming his mind towards oblivion.

With the intent of a mad man, he races down Interstate 5. No one dares stop him. Men in leather and on Hogs pull over and watch, admiring the sound of thunder—of over 650 British hooves—pounding the pavement. The road becomes pliable under the tread of his tires. Two Kawazaki Ninjas slow down as he passes. An old man on a Goldwing waves and spits.

Dairy Exit appears.

Last Exit before Mexico.

Signs warn of pedestrian families attempting to cross the highway illegally.

Barbed wire appears on brick walls.

Cars pile up at the border crossing, each one fighting with the other to edge ahead by inches. Horns honk. Exhaust fouls the air. Middle fingers flip off other fingers. The Triumph hugs the cement wall perilously, the toe of Ted's left boot only inches away. Shadows leap out at him, hissing, chanting, laughing. Like a fool, perhaps like a rodeo clown toying with a bull, he darts in and out of traffic. Front bumpers, like horns, attempt to gore him.

A thin corrugated sign, only inches thick. A cement barricade, less than a foot. An overpass. Suddenly, the United States stops—no ceremony, no band, no rites, no great natural boundary, great valley or canyon, not even a drummer boy to keep time to the wind whispered *corridos*. The mightiest nation on earth just stops.

The Mexican border guards waved him on, smiling, flashing their coca stained teeth. He didn't need their permission to enter. Nor did he need a passport. Didn't he notice the jaguar patches on their shoulders? What about their snake leather boots and belts?

Kiosk stands lined the other side, begging the returning gringos and Chicanos to purchase more kitsch than they needed. Small Indian children darted like matadors between the stalled traffic, their young tender lungs blackened by exhaust, selling lizard and serpent masks. Old Indian men with cowboy hats attempted to pawn jaguar figurines. An old Indian woman, playing with five marionettes, spat laughter as Ted roared past.

Ted's mind shut out the activities of the other side. He noticed nothing. The Triumph continued to roar, hurling him onwards. A sign: Rosarita. He followed it past dirt soccer fields and bronze statues of Aztec warriors.

Racing along the border, did he notice the graffiti that lined the new military styled corrugated fence? Did he note the small pink and baby blue adobe houses on the opposite side? What about the hundreds who lined up to cross to the lure of *El Norte*—the New Testament's mythical Canaan? "*Ai*," dark shadows beneath the rocks hissed in warning, "*Las apariencias engañan.*" No one appeared to take heed. Ted's Triumph roared past. Bluish smoke lingered in its wake.

The Triumph's heavy knobbed tires rolled through patches of semi-dried water, sewage that had recently spilled onto the street. Strange sweet odors assaulted his nose. Still, he felt relieved.

Reaching the top of the hill, he jumped the curb and stopped. Dust rose about him. Removing his helmet, he breathed deeply. Somewhere across the valley, he reflected, is San Diego County. Beyond that—Los Angeles. And beyond that—Santa Cruz. Between them is a no man's wasteland: border patrolmen in green Chevy blazers; helicopters that patrol the air like wasps.

Relief flooded through him at the feel of having entered another world. What of Stagecoach City? Of Studio Mictlan? Was that what the wind had been hissing in his ears during the last two mad hours?

Revving the Triumph's engine, and turning south, Ted pulled back out onto the highway and rumbled off. Borderlanders stopped. Some were perched on top of the fence. Others sat at its base, eating corn tortillas. Some were caught crawling through punctured holes. Others were hiding under rocks. Eyes watched and ears listened as smoke filled the air. The sun's brilliance flashed off the Triumph's white gas tank. Everyone sneered. Tongues wagged at him. The Triumph's roar drowned out their hissing.

Southernlands

On the road. Leaving his canoe at the beach, Tez followed the road to the top of the hill. Below him, and across the lake, stood the two great sister cities of Tenochtitlan and Tlatlelolco. But his brother was lost to him forever. His mother, too. And his father had never been there. Sadness and longing for what could not be filled his heart.

Since childhood he had been prepared to accept his fate, to know that if he were caught and sacrificed on the stone alter he would be offering his blood for both those he loved and the entire cosmos. But he had never been prepared to face the loss of his family, or the disruption of the divine plan of the ages. Alone, and ashamed by his own lack of courage, he felt he could not place the crown of Toxcatl upon his head. Moreover, how could he face his friends, Atototl, Quiauhxochitl, and Matlalxochitl, make love with them, share the last days of his life with them, if he was full of fear?

He knew how intense the time with them would be. They would go beyond lovemaking. They would attempt to unmask him, to discover what was really within him, to know if he were truly worthy. Only courage and total acceptance of his fate would make his offering truly propitious—anything less than that would be just an empty skin. He would rather flee, as a coward, as a man without a people—forever disgraced, then have to watch as they slowly, day by day, and night by night, under each tender kiss, uncovered his innermost feelings of fear and resentment.

Looking back at his city, tears filled his eyes as he took in for the last time the images of temples and palaces rising like mountaintops above the lake.

CHAPTER 11

❀

Southernlands

Tenochtitlan. Disease struck the inhabitants with wrath. Everywhere, people lay dying, their bodies covered with boils, their eyes blinded. No one buried the dead.

Priests cried out to the gods, bleeding themselves, offering the healthy. The gods, however, remained silent. "Perhaps they are dead?" lamented a lone mad priest from his mountain cave. Women and children died. Warriors died. Even the royal palace was not spared. Like a shadow, like a serpent slithering amongst the reeds, death itself crept up and struck the new Emperor Cuitlauac, filling his veins with venom, turning the hue of his blood dark.

The surviving lords gathered in the royal palace. Their bodies were marked. Pus oozed from their wounds. Smoke filled their eyes and nostrils. Now they knew. Now they understood. Word had already reached their ears. The final chapter in their destiny was upon them. The Sun, that imperfect unbalanced Sun, was finally dying, tottering off its course. No amount of precious fluid could restore it. The warriors and priests had failed. The wizards had failed. Moctezuma had failed. Cuitlauac had failed. The monsters of the twilight, the Locusts, had arrived. They had walked amongst them. They had eaten both gods and gold. Teleos had finally arrived, in all its terror and horror, without mercy, without compassion. The cosmos itself, the great void, had opened its mouth and was devouring the Sun.

The lords looked at each other. There was no doubt. The eagle had fallen. Cuahutemoc, chosen for his lineage, courage, and namesake, would be appointed to bring the world to its end.

*   *   *

The Center of the world. There was no time for fasting. Nor was there time for seclusion. Stripping himself naked, the Emperor-elect marched to the throne and accepted his new duties with great trepidation.

How would he rule? he wondered. Most of his people were dead or dying. The Sun was being swallowed. The gold had been eaten. The high priests had died of exhaustion, bleeding themselves to death. The King of Toxcatl had not been sacrificed. There was no one left who was healthy enough to merit being offered to Huitzilopotzli.

Walking to the top of the temple, sadness filled his soul as he looked out over his city. His gaze moved across the lake. His foes were advancing. His friends had abandoned him. Trade was shriveling to but a pittance of what it had been. The great merchants, mighty in arms, had vanished, taking their merchandise with them. Hunger had long since taken up its abode in Tenochtitlan.

Borderlands

In the mountains. Standing upon a ledge high above the valley, Tez watched as the army approached. From his perspective, they looked like millions of ants gathering at the lakeside. What invisible hand was guiding them? he wondered.

His vision returned to the mountainside he was now upon, and then retraced his journey. He followed the narrow winding dirt road down to the sand, to the army of voracious ants and their Locust gods, to the water, across the water to the island, to Mexico itself.

Tenochtitlan and its sister Tlatelolco stood silent, like two enchanting adulteresses, awaiting their destiny. No smoke arose from the city. No drumbeats could be heard. Nothing seemed to move. It was as if life itself were about to be vanquished. Moreover, Tez realized, despite the Sun's angle, the sister cities' reflections were barely visible on the lake's surface.

Was Tez happy that he had escaped—that he had managed to avoid his people's fate? Or did guilt pervade him? Like a man struck with paralysis by the goddesses of the night, those valorous women who had died in childbirth, he stood watching, caught at the juncture of time and space. Slowly, very slowly, the Sun stole what was left of the two sister-cities' glorious reflections and began to set.

Turning his back on the spectacle, Tez steps north, to the land of origins.

Southernlands

Tenochtitlan. The newly appointed high priest found the Emperor Cuauhtemoc alone and in meditation within his palace. Looking up, the Emperor motioned for the high priest to sit across from him. For some time, neither spoke. Darkness and smoke filled the room.

"How long, oh lord, has it been since you've left the palace and walked amongst your people?"

Cuahutemoc did not answer. He accepted the condemnation, knowing that the burden of his people's fate had fallen upon him.

"I have ventured out, my friend," Cuahutemoc finally retorted, drawing in his breath. "Once so full of noble people, the city now lies humbled, alone in our aloneness. Were we not the power among nations? The heirs of the Toltecs?"

"Yes, my lord," the high priest answered. "Once, Tenochtitlan was queen over the mighty. Now, like a poor widow, like a woman who has seen her beloved stung to death by scorpions, she laments both day and night. Alas, of all her allies there is none to aid her."

"Her friends have turned to foes," the Emperor added. "Her gates are all deserted, and her remaining priests despair. Her lovely maidens, the pleasures of spring, have been dragged away and are now held captive."

"Bitter is her lot."

"Her foes have surrounded her. Hunger pangs assault her."

"Her enemies of old and new exalt in her humiliation."

"Was not jealousy always part of their plot?"

"Her leader—you—oh lord, are like a stag. Your enemies drive you before them. Their dogs chase you with pleasure, howling as you flee. Your hooves have become ensnared in branches, covered with rot."

"All who had honored her despise her now. Bitter is our lot."

"Yes. Bitter is *your* lot, oh lord."

"Filth clings to our quetzal feathers. Our silver lies tarnished. Our gold has been eaten."

"Even worse, oh lord, your magic is powerless to restrain the tragic."

"All my people are groaning in their search for food, moaning in the afflictions of their skin. No sweet balm can purify them. No herb can restore them. Who am I? Who am I?"

"The Captain of the Locusts sent a fever to waste your cousin's limbs; he spread a net to catch your feet; he destroyed the great Moctezuma with deceit; bound a yoke about his neck, cursed is he now by all Toltec."

"A bitter lot is ours. All our heroes flouted; all our warriors routed. He cried out to our old allies…"

"You are mistaken, oh great lord. Your cousin did not cry out. No one abandoned him. No one failed him. As the first among men, he accepted his fate."

"Then why, oh Moctezuma, are your priests dying of hunger? Your few remaining warriors cannot persevere," Cuahutemoc cried.

"Your tonal is wretched, your heart is writhing and your vitals burn—all of your high priest have suggested."

"Outside, the Locusts have gathered. Inside, the plague. The jaguar feasts upon both the Sun and the Moon," the high priest continued.

"My strongholds have been shattered. Bitter is my lot."

"Do you bemoan your fate, oh lord? Would you prefer to postpone?"

"You speak of avoiding my fate? Why should my heart not melt? Babies and infants swoon in the streets, sucking at the dry breasts of their dead mothers' corpses, their tiny lungs gasping."

"Across the lake stands both former friends and foes, hissing with glee. Listen!"

"They cup their hands about their mouths and mock me, 'So this is the great beauty, the joy of all the earth?' Oh, bitter is her lot."

"What was planned long ago is now being carried out."

"Tears stream throughout the day."

"Do you rise and cry with the priests at night, oh lord?"

"I have seen women gnawing on the bones of the children they once cuddled. The bodies of priests clutter the temples. No one removes them. My cousin's skin and flesh was worn away. How dare you accuse me of going astray!"

"Bitter lot was his. Moctezuma, too, was bound with chains. His life was ended in great pain."

"And I dwell in the dark, like a man long dead, entombed and bled, continually misled."

"How long, oh lord, shall you avoid the setting of the Sun? Shall you continue, like a fool, to search for reprieve?"

"It is a sight that I cannot bear, the jaguar's final stare."

"What you seek you shall not receive. Bitter, I repeat, bitter is your lot."

"The entire cosmos fulminates against me. Leave me now, and tarry not."

"Remember, oh great lord, your fate. Drink deeply, for the Locusts' final sting must be sought."

"Oh, truly bitter is my lot."

Borderlands

Tijuana. The Triumph continued to roar, burning up the road, traveling south. Reaching the top of a hill, the ocean came into view. Two islands loomed just off the coast, uninhabited. Do seamen still visit them, docking their boats? Had they ever been pregnant with life? Why are there no cathedrals and casinos? Ted failed to wonder.

The road continued on towards Rosarita and Ensenada. One sign, to the right, read *Playas.* Ted hesitated, relaxing the throttle. The Triumph backfired. Young birds rose from bushes, their wings fluttering, frightened.

Playas. The word echoed in his mind. *Playas?* At the last moment, the Triumph swerved, its rider barely hanging on.

Playas. Ted could feel the heat of the Triumph's four-stroke engine through his leather boots and jeans. He knew that if he were to touch the engine, the skin on his hands would instantly blister. If he held on, his flesh would melt from his bones.

The journey from Stagecoach City to Playas had been tough. The Triumph's constant vibration had numbed both hands. His back hurt. His right hand and forearm ached from holding the throttle. His ass hurt. His legs pained him. The saddle had cut off the circulation to his loin—leaving his crotch numb. Was he out of condition? Had he spent too many years—or was it aeons—trapped within Studio Mictlan?

All roads in *Playas* lead to one point: the bullfighting arena. By the time Ted reached the arena, he was exhausted. His dry throat ached.

Pulling up in front of the deserted auditorium, he gazed at the sight of the bronze bull and matador. Wonder and terror filled him. A strange sensation he had perhaps once known and forgotten reverberated through him.

Small *niños* jumped out of shadows, wanting to examine the Triumph—his Triumph. Revving its mighty horses, Ted roared off, leaving the *niños* and their *madres* aghast.

Aimlessly, he circled the arena. Was it four times or seven? Perhaps nine? He had lost count.

Each time he passed, his eyes remained riveted on the bull and the matador. The bull's muscles bulged. Who can match his strength? His fury? The power of his loins? Next to him stood the matador, the merchant of death, full of grace. Who can avoid his sword?

As he continued to circle, images of the mindless crowds, the drunken crowds, the insincere and unworthy crowds, feverishly cheering the spectacle of the bull and matador in their dance with fate and death, haunted him.

The bull, Ted pondered. The tragedy. Tears. Understanding? Its body bloodied from spears, fury in its eyes, snorting fire, phallus erect, pounding the ground with its hoofs—thundering, charging death, charging the sword. Does it not, in its final charge, with all its might and ferocity, evoke…?

A lone street behind the arena. A boardwalk? He pulled away from the arena and entered the last street, his Triumph roaring, spitting, snorting. That place where the pavement meets dirt, where dirt turns to sand, where the sand stretches out to the surf, where the surf stops, where the water reaches the ends of Mexico.

Southernlands

Tenochtitlan. The wind blew gently across the lake's water. The sun blazed overhead, mocking those below. Cuahutemoc and his warriors stepped into their canoes and paddled towards the middle of the lake. From the other side, the Captain of the Locusts, clad in white, a belt of gold around his waist, his eyes flashing with fire, his feet shod with bronze, ordered his men and Locusts to launch their brigantines.

❦   ❦   ❦

The Center. Canoe met brigantine in the center of the lake. The conqueror's voice echoed like the sound of waves. The Emperor drew himself up and faced his foe.

"I have given you time to repent, yet you continue to refuse," the Captain hissed, his serpent's tongue finally loosed. All were amazed to hear him speak.

"I ask you, do you repent of your sins?" he hissed again, his tongue flicking back and forth between his lips.

Cuauhtemoc remained silent, staring, his eyes unflinching.

"Look, oh Mexicans! With me is a great host, which no man can count, from every nation and tribe and people and tongue. Do you still refuse to repent?"

Cuauhtemoc kept his posture.

"I have given them the power to kill your men with weapons and famine and plague and by wild beasts of both heaven, earth and sea. Only a fool would refuse. Surrender now and spare your lives."

And then the leaders of the seven nations—Tlaxcala, Texcoco, Azt-capotzalco, Chichen Itza, Tlacophan, Cuauhtitlan, Xilote-pec—remonstrated with one voice, "Oh great Captain, how long will you refrain from avenging our blood upon those who dwell in Tenochtitlan?"

"Have no fear, my brothers. I shall shepherd them with an iron rod, shattering them like potters' jars. All your enemies shall wail because of me. I have given you the power to shut up the heavens that no rain shall fall on your enemies. I have given you the strength to smite the earth with plagues. Now I give you the rights over waters, to turn it to blood and drown every soul."

With that the lords of the nations shouted with joy.

Another Locust stepped forward, hissing and holding a book above his head: "Written in this book are the names of all your enemies. Whoever is destined for captivity, to captivity he goes! And whoever is destined for death, to death he goes!"

Again, the lords raised their spears with cries of jubilation.

Then a second Locust stepped forward, hissing to the gathered hosts: "Fear our Captain and give him glory, for the final hour, the great judgment, is upon us!"

And again all the lords bellowed with joy.

Then a third Locust stepped forward, pointing at the new Emperor Cuauhutemoc and his men, hissing: "Tenochtitlan the great has fallen! The city that made all nations drink of her lusts. Our Captain's anger is poured out upon her! The smoke of her torments shall rise forever and ever! No rest shall she receive by day or by night!"

And again the lords clamored with jubilation.

Then a fourth Locust stepped forward and hissed: "Tenochtitlan is but a house of demons now, a den of foul spirits, a cage of loathsome creatures, a temple of harlots. All nations have drunk from her passion. The kings of all the earth have committed adultery with her. And by her the earth's merchants have grown rich. She has fallen!"

And again the lords shouted with joy.

Then the Locusts kneeled before their Captain, chanting and hissing in unison:

"Great and marvelous are your deeds,
righteous and true your ways!
All shall kneel before you.
Deserved and true your sentences of doom!"

Opening his mouth, the Captain of the Locusts shouted: "I am the one who was, and who is, and who is coming! This is my last warning: Come out of her my people, if you do not wish to share in her final afflictions."

The Captain's words struck fear and terror in the hearts of the gathered Aztec warriors. Their will began to break. Every eye turned upon Cuauhutemoc, pleading for guidance.

His eyes held the Captain's steady gaze. They searched each other's souls, probing, exploring. He felt the darkness of the Locust's heart and his own strength fading. It was as if his very life force, his tonal, was being sucked out of him. Something within him cried out to surrender. Images of his beloved cousin Moctezuma, chained, humiliated and imprisoned, flooded his mind.

One of his commanders leaned over and hissed in his ears, "Look at them, my Lord. Power and strength have they. Who can count their numbers? Like the grains of the sand are they. What chances do we have? Only a fool would fight."

With each word, each syllable, he felt his will receding into the water's depths. And yet, his eyes never left the Captain's.

"Come out of her my people!" the Captain repeated.

Several warriors leaped from their canoes and swam to the brigantines, joining the giant federation. They were greeted with shouts and embraces. Old friends reunited. The Emperor's power continued to diminish. More men abandoned him. Hundreds. Feebly, he attempted to steady himself on his quivering legs. The canoe rocked. The sea opened, waiting to receive him into its depths.

Then, slowly, like a priest recovering from an extended fast, like a wizard returning from the other side, like a clubbed warrior rising to his feet, like a young child taking its first steps, he leaned slowly forward. A small ache, beginning in his toes, and traveling up through his legs and torso, began to pulse within him, and then turned to pounding. His fists clenched and unclenched. Everyone took notice. His left leg moved first. His right leg followed. Like a newborn colt, he tottered about on the canoe, trying to get his feet under him.

The Captain's eyes searched his foe's soul. Suddenly, he understood and smiled.

Like a young lion, wounded and bloodied by his opponent, Cuauhutemoc shook his mane. His long hair flew from side to side, shattering the spell. Opening his mouth, he roared with fury, vengeance, and the jubilation of the hunt.

The Captain greeted his roar with a mighty hiss. Their eyes met again, sizing each other, smirking. Each understood that the release of their own potential now was in the other's hands.

"Anyone who wishes to join the Captain and his federation of nations may do so. I, for my part, shall return to the city of our forefathers and await that which has been decreed from the beginning," the young lion announced, taking the oar and beginning to paddle back towards shore.

No one moved. Thousands upon thousands of gathered warriors on both sides watched the lone canoe as it made its way back towards the island. Only the Captain of the Locusts smiled, his eyes dancing with respect.

Then, slowly, one canoe at a time, the Aztec heroes turned and followed their king.

The Captain of the Locusts raised his stinger threateningly, preventing anyone from attacking the Aztecs as they retreated. Longing and admiration filled his soul. Then, dropping to one knee, he hissed words that no man could understand.

When the last canoe had reached the island, the Captain stood up, turned to his men, raised his stinger high into the air and hissed with a thousand tongues: "Tenochtitlan the great has fallen! Now we call her to account for her misdeeds. The final hour has arrived. Render to her what she rendered to others! Double the cup of her doom. Mix her twice the drink of death that she portioned out to others. Just as she gloried and played, reveling in her luxuries, give her like torment and tears. Pestilence! Agony! Famine! And death! Let her burn with fire! Let none of you wail for her, lest you feel my wrath!"

Then the entire federation of warriors, ten thousand times ten thousand, with their spears raised in the air, chanted, their voices shaking the earth itself, causing the lake's water to foam:

"Great city!

Strong city!

In one hour you shall meet your doom!"

Spreading his wings, long stingers in each hand, the Captain of the Locusts cried out with all his might. His voice, melodious and wonderful, carried across the lake, echoing throughout the city, taking up residence in every shadow: "Behold! I am coming over the waters, riding upon the clouds. Every eye shall see me. Even those who have forsaken me! And every knee shall bow."

Borderlands

Playas. The sun shone brightly overhead. Sitting upon his Triumph, one boot on the ground, the great white beast tilting slightly, its handlebars threatening like horns, Ted stared at the wall of unaesthetic gray corrugated steel sheets. At least eight feet high, it rent the earth and separated mankind.

Old washed out graffiti—strange slogans, faded Olmec faces, aborted fetuses, eagles and snakes, skulls and crosses—stared back at him.

Years ago—perhaps in another life—he had been to Berlin, a stopover on his way to 'Nam. He had seen the Wall, peered over it towards America's Evil Empire. Like all GIs, he too had left his mark one night, drunk on Bavarian beer and Rhine wine. Vomiting and pissing, terrified beyond belief, he had scrawled his name. It too, that great concrete Berlin Wall, had cut the earth in half, separating family and friends.

And yet, strangely enough, despite the fact that this fence lacked the tanks, the Russians, cloaked KGB and hooded CIA, the whole nuclear arsenal of the two sister Wests, it was far more eerie: alone, alienated, terrifying. The great corrugated steel gate to shattered memories and new dreams.

Ted shuttered. He had never seen anything like it. And yet, he had lived only hours from it, from the last frontier. What scent did it have? What rites of passage did it demand? Why must one crawl under it, through mud and stickers, over rattlers, scorpions, and black widows, past bandits, murderers, tourists, and police? The awful initiation of horror that the North demanded from the South—an initiation without reward. "*A veces querer no es poder,*" the lizards warn from beneath the shrubs to the endless stream of "illegals" as they move in slow, methodical and endless waves towards the siren's call, the thin green line, the beacon's lights, the jagged and bloodied rocks before the shore.

His gaze traveled the length of the steel fence. A straight shot down the hill, across the sand, and into the sea. Feebly, it parted the waves. Was it attempting to separate the water? Waves pushed against it and over it. It stretched out into the ocean. Twenty mad, absurd, feet and then stopped.

Ted walked down the hill, his focus never leaving that point where the worlds met and ended.

Leaving his boots and socks on the rocky hill, he dug his bare toes into the sand. Did it feel like the sand he remembered in Santa Cruz? At Newport Beach? Huntington Beach? He wasn't sure.

The cold Pacific Ocean numbed his feet. He looked out at the two dead islands and wondered. Stretching, he turned north and stared up the coast, at the deserted Imperial Beaches.

The water slapped his ankles and legs. The surf slapped at the wet sand. Something else...? His ear caught it. A faint sound. He hesitated. He did not turn and look. Why? Then he recognized it—the sound of a sandal slapping against a sole.

"Nopoles?" the plump Mestizo asked him, her face scarred by acne.

"Nopoles, Mr.?" she repeated.

"No, gracias." Ted said, impressed with his command of Spanish.

His eyes traveled the length of her rotund body. Had he ever seen an obese person on the beach before? He couldn't recall. She seemed different, somehow, from the northern obese. How? Wasn't there something natural about her? Was she less grotesque? Or even grotesque at all? He followed her walk, listening to the sounds of surf and sandal slapping in harmony, his stare fixed on her huge breasts and hips, gently dancing with every step.

He watched her walk through the sand, her thighs rubbing against each other, her legs struggling to propel her against the tide. Was her ass pickled with cellulose? His mind wandered. Memories of images—faint images—clouds and stones…

Beyond her stood his Triumph, calling silently for him to return from the absurd. Lowering his gaze, he followed her back to the last street, his eyes riveted to her duck like waddle, welcoming him to wherever it was that he now stood.

*   *   *

The boardwalk. Small family owned kiosks lined the last street, the backs of their huts closed and turned against the water and deserted islands. Ted strolled the length of the boardwalk, inspecting the wares. Some sold coconuts; others sold fish. Some offered ice cream, others soda. Only one kiosk, the last one on the row, sold alcohol.

Seating himself upon an old metal outdoor barstool, rusted brown by the sea, Ted waited for a menu.

He was surrounded by several old men. Why weren't there any younger men? he wondered. No one seemed to notice him. No one offered to serve him. Was it because he was from over there? *El Norte*? Anger began to rise in him. All he wanted was a fucking beer! his mind cried.

A man, not much older than himself, most of one arm missing, walked from out of the shadows. Ted tried not to stare at the stump.

"What do you want?" he asked, his accent more Chicano than Mexican, Ted noted. He was wearing well-ironed, pleated, beige dress pants, a loose white cut T-shirt, and a knitted ski cap on his head.

"Hi." Ted hesitated, hoping that he wouldn't have to shake hands.

"I'll take a beer. Dos XX," he said, wondering what a Cholo was doing in Mexico.

The bartender looked at him and smiled. His face was marked by acne. Ted couldn't help but traverse the terrible lunar-like terrain with his eyes. Red. Rough. Had the boils pussed? He looked away. The man said something to the bartender. Was it in Spanish?

The bartender replied, the melody of his voice somehow strange. But this was Mexico, wasn't it?

"No beer. Sorry," the man shrugged. Ted glanced at the man's good arm, his wickedly muscular arm. A tattoo, faded and gray, was etched into his shoulder. *Angel.* Typical Chicano bullshit, Ted thought.

"Nice bike. You're the first gringo we've ever seen on this street. They usually don't get down this far. Parking lot and that's it. They come here for the dog races. Most never even get past *La marqueta.*"

"What else do you have?"

"This ain't no bar man. This here's a *patecatl.* What gives you the right to trespass, man?" he mumbled to himself, his voice barely carrying above a feint.

"I'm sorry…?"

"Oh, man. A *patecatl.* In the North, they drink wheat and grapes. In the South, they drink cactus. This ain't South. And it sure ain't North. So we drink the drink of patecatl."

"Which is?"

"You ever heard of astyanax? Kicks harder than a mule in heat! Try it."

"All right," Ted said, accepting the challenge.

The man said something to the bartender. Again, everyone laughed. An old man sat down across from him, his fingers gnarled with age. Ted felt uncomfortable under the old man's stare. When he looked over, the old man smiled, revealing blackened and missing teeth—teeth that had been lost from malnutrition? Teeth that had been knocked out in back alley fights? Ted stared into the dark cavernous hole.

"So, what's your name? Let me guess, Angel?" Ted ventured, tearing his eyes away from the old man and feeling suddenly froggy.

"*Chingao?!*" he smirked, suddenly looking dangerous despite his missing appendage.

"Juan. Juan Manuel," he said, the crow's feet around his eyes relaxing.

"Hey Juan. I'm Ted."

The bartender slid the shot glass of astyanax across the wooden bar. It looked like whiskey. Ted took a sip.

"Jesus Christ!" he exclaimed, coughing. "You were right."

The old man took out a cigar, staring hard at Ted.

"Don't mind that old man," Juan said. "But he's got the three prettiest *chavalas* you ever saw. Uhm um. Tits like coconuts. It'll make your heart bleed."

"Is that right?" Ted asked, taking another sip.

"So, what's a gringo like you doing here, anyway?"

"Long story."

"Do you speak any *español?*"

"A little. But I have difficulties with the Mexican accent. In school, we were taught…"

The old man spit.

"*Adonde vas?* Where are you going?"

"I don't know. South, I guess. Maybe…"

The fat woman he had seen on the beach walked over and stood next to Juan, placing a swollen hand on his shoulder.

"Where you gonna stay, man? Tonight, I mean?"

"I don't know," Ted replied, looking at the heavyset woman's scarred face.

"Hey. I can fix you up. You wanna get laid? I know some nice ladies," he said, patting the woman's rear. "Clean. No shit, man. Clean. Ain't nobody but me had their pecker in them for years. Whata you say? The first rounds on me."

Taking another sip of his drink, looking at Juan and the fat lady, the potion burning his throat, glowing in his stomach, he considered the offer. The fat lady smiled. Could she understand English? Ted wondered. Should he feel embarrassed? Why was he toying with the idea? Was it to amuse himself—with the absurdity of it?

"Clean? How clean?"

"Doctor certified and all that shit. Pedigreed. Whata you say?"

The old man, puffing smoke into the air, and watching the transaction from where he sat, laughed and coughed until he spat black ooze onto the floor.

"Hell, I don't know. Reminds me of Nam."

"Look at you. I can tell. Your peckers been rottin' for years, man. Am I right? You probably haven't gotten it since back then—Vietnam, right? Yeah, that's what I thought. So, are you up for it? A kind of adios to America, to what you left behind—just like in Saigon. Come on man. What have you got to lose? You're not a virgin, are you? I got virgins. I got them all, man. Girls. Beautiful girls. Tits out to here! Girls, man. Girls! First round's free. I'll even throw in another girl. You can fuck two at a time. No. Make it three. You up for three? Shit. How about four, friend? Are you hung like a bull? Do you have the balls? Balls like melons? Four girls. Four! All at one time, friend. You won't be able to walk again. Forget your bike, man. No more sitting. No way. Whata you say, bro?"

"You're not pimping, are you?" Ted said, laughing

"Do I look like a pimp? Shit. I'm a priest, man. What does the tattoo say? *Angel*, right? Check this out!" he commanded, pulling up his shirt and revealing a giant red crucifix. "Come on, bro? Can your filthy gringo cock handle four? Four! Four ladies, bro! Right now. Four ladies to fuck you and suck you, drive you insane, from every direction: north, south, east, and west!"

"First round's free?"

"First round, bro. Satisfaction guaranteed. I'll even give you some skin."

Taking another drink, cigar smoke filling the room, clouding his mind, choking his throat, he pondered the proposition.

"Let me see the girls first," he finally said, teasing himself. After all, he could always back out, couldn't he?

"That's my bro." Juan said, his voice suddenly full of affection.

❧   ❧   ❧

On the boardwalk. Juan ordered another glass of astyanax. Clanging their shot glasses together, the two men gulped the burning fluid. Soon, the bartender placed a bottle on the table. Both men laughed and drank. The barstool bucked like a bronco.

Standing up, Ted tottered about, unsure of his legs, his mind clouded, his voice emitting uncontrolled giggles between his slurred speech. He was surprised to see that his friend—what was his name?—seemed unaffected by the drink. Why? Was it because he was accustomed to drinking astyanax, a seasoned skipper, sure of his legs?

The two men walked back up the boardwalk towards the threatening gray wall. The old man with the Cuban cigar trailed behind.

Someone pissed against it. Was it Ted? Was he that drunk? Did nausea overwhelm him, too? Did his stomach vacuum itself of its contents?

Juan ponied onto the Triumph. Taking it by the handlebars and jumping up, he kicked the starter with all his might. Instantly, the beast roared into being. Ted swung his right leg over the saddle, plopping down behind Juan. Popping the clutch, the beast's front tire raised up off the ground, leaving the wall behind. Ted hung on to his newfound companion.

The old man watched, smiling, as they raced off. Cigar smoke enshrouded him.

The bordello. Ted had no idea where it was that Juan had taken him. He figured it was some sort of borderland brothel, but he couldn't be sure. His mind was still spinning from asythanax. He had lost track of time. Had Juan assured him that it would soon clear? Had Juan taken the direct route to the brothel? Ted looked about for an orientation. Wasn't that the wall over there? Had they ended up at the place where they had begun? What kind of wild ride had he been taken on, anyway? Had they just prowled the streets of Tijuana for the hell of it, without purpose, just to feel the roar and might of their Triumph?

The two-story house seemed out of place among the surrounding destitution. Indian women looked on as the beast rumbled into the village. Mestizo boys, playing futbal, hesitated. Ted's mind began to clear. An old Indian woman peered at him and laughed. A crowd of serious looking Indians began to gather. Had they been waiting for him? Taking hold of his triceps, Juan tugged at him, urging him towards the gaudy pink house.

The old man with the cigar was standing on the porch, smiling and smoking as they approached. Ted walked past him, wondering. A loud squalor began to arise from the quickly growing crowd of gathered Indians. The courtyard door shut behind them.

They walked single file through the courtyard. A statue of Michael the Archangel defeating the Great Dragon stood in the northern corner, beside Our Lady. A cactus garden, overflowing with fruit, was located against the southern wall. A fountain stood in the middle, splashing water. Ted hesitated, considering the beauty of the fountain. Reaching down, he dipped his hand into the water. Inhaling deeply, the old man's cigar glowed with fury. Ashes fell onto Ted's exposed neck, burning his skin. Reaching into the fountain, Juan, too, placed his hand into its water. The two men eyed each other. Juan splashed, laughing. Ted enjoyed the feel of the cool water as it sprayed his face and head. The old man exhaled. Smoke bathed Ted and Juan. The two men laughed like boys, their blood filled with drink.

"*Chavalas*," Juan whispered, slapping Ted on the back, "pretty enough for a king."

"Babes!" Ted laughed.

The old door was slightly jammed. A quick kick and Juan had it open. Ted followed.

He never heard the blow. He took the shot between his shoulder blades. His lungs gasped. His breath expelled. For an instant, his mind cleared. Then his vision, his entire perception, vanished.

Southernlands

On the island. The beaches shook under the steady barrage of earth rending cannon fire. Smoke rose from the brigantines. The stench of sulfur permeated the air. Cuahutemoc gathered his remaining troops. The women had been removed to the sister city, Tlatelolco. There, for the first time, they too were preparing for battle.

Cuauhutemoc considered his companions. Were they afraid? Were they prepared? How had they spent their last night? Had lovers felt each other's passion one last time before parting? Had father's said goodbye to their sons? Had mothers steadied themselves against the thought of their daughters' cries as the Locusts drag them away to their black islands?

Time slowed as his eyes swept over his remaining troops.

Distant drumbeats announced that the destroyers had landed. Shaking his mane he raised his spear high above his head. Opening his mouth, he roared. Several thousand roars joined his, shaking both temples and heavens.

Every eye remained riveted on him. Elders wondered. What were his plans? How would he bring the tragedy to its end? Young men considered him, proud to serve under him. Falling Eagle—the last Emperor of the Aztecs. There was no doubt. No hesitation.

He took a step and stopped. His men followed. He took another step and jumped. His troops followed. He kicked and twirled. So did they. He shook his head. So did they. It was a new step. None they had ever known. He taught them the final dance. A procession. No great. No small. They jumped and kicked and twirled. A drummer caught the rhythm and kept time. An owl, the Quetzal Owl, joined the dance, hooting. The last dance.

Together, tears clouding their eyes—tears of?

The destroyers entered the city, led by their Captain. The earth shook beneath their march. Locusts charged, stingers raised. Mighty gods galloped towards them. Foul dogs snarled and snapped, their powerful jaws threatening to crush limbs. Former friends and foes raised spears and clubs, shouting with approval. And yet, still they danced.

Like men drunk for the first time, they danced and tottered about—twirling, kicking and somersaulting. Cauhutemoc continued to lead. With great joy they closed the space between them, triumphantly engaging the destroyer—finally meeting their god.

Borderlands

The bordello. The room is dark. He feels the cold stone under his bare feet. Who has removed his boots? He touches his legs. Where are his pants? He is naked. Silently, he waits. His mind has become clear.

Someone enters the room. Ted cannot see. Is he blind? Has the astyanax destroyed his vision? Candles are lit one by one. The room glows. Shadows leap about the room, dancing on the ceiling and walls. A small figure steps forward. His mind spins. Moku? he wants to cry. His throat is dry. His mouth won't open. She takes his hand. He does not resist. His ear catches the sound of heavy bare feet slapping the stone floor. He turns. Dite? Shock overcomes him. She takes his other hand. Someone steps out of the shadow. Shaking her long mane, she stands before him, eyeing his naked candlelit body.

The spell is broken. Ted fights, wrenching his arms free. The two women step back, watching, enjoying. Ted rises to his feet. Like a pugilist, he circles clockwise. The woman with the mane falls into step with him. He throws a jab at her. She hesitates and then inches to the left, letting his blow slip past her. Wind hisses in her ears, heightening the game. He throws a looping cross, hoping to break her nose. She dances to her left. The blow falls harmlessly over her left shoulder. She steps beyond him, moving past him.

More candles are lit. Shadows dance. Again, with all his might, he throws a left hook, anticipating that he will crush her skull. Like a nymph, she moves under his force, stepping again to the left. His momentum carries him on. A quick right uppercut to the ribs propels him forward. Her sharp claws have ripped his flesh. Losing his balance, he falls.

The cold stone floor greets him. Warm blood fills his mouth. He turns, rolling over. She squats before him, eyeing him, growling.

He raises himself onto his hands and knees. Can he stand up? If only he could hit her squarely! Someone else steps out of the shadows. He looks up. Her clothes fall about her ankles. He remembers her naked body. She dances in front of him, growling and kicking. He crawls towards her, lunging at her feet. She dances away and stops.

Sweat fills his vision. Rubbing his eyes, he watches as she places a pair of high-heeled shoes—stilettos—onto her feet. He hears the sound of the two spikes against the stone floor. He crawls towards her. Can he catch hold of an ankle? Trip her? Get his hands on her throat? His mind is blank with rage. Someone jumps over him. He punches at the air. The naked witch on spikes dances before him. He continues crawling towards her. A sharp sidekick hits his right eye. His vision—blood and pus begin to flow, dripping onto the stone.

He tries to stand. A sharp kick to the groin doubles him over. A brutal knee crashing into his face hurls him onto his back. He lands spread eagle.

Hands take hold of his arms and legs, lifting him off the floor. He attempts to struggle. He cannot free himself.

The old man enters, still smoking his cigar. He peers at Ted's naked body, puffing and blowing smoke. He places something on Ted's head. Ted struggles in vain, unable to break free from their wicked grasp.

His right eye is lost. He peers with his remaining eye. His vision has become two-dimensional and blurred. Yet, he sees Juan standing over him, his missing stump of an arm dangling about in the dark. Shadows dance across his scarred skin. Ted looks up at the dark ceiling. The candlelight flickers against it, teasing him with images of places he believes he has never been or seen. Ted's vision moves to the man's arm. *Angel.* His eye traverses the deformity—from shoulder to elbow to forearm to hand.

Terror takes hold of his mind. He has seen it. He wants to scream. Panic seizes him. Someone kisses his forehead tenderly. Their eyes meet. Slowly, mysteriously, quiet takes possession of him. His mind does not comprehend why. Somehow—another gentle kiss—a distant breeze. Now he understands. His body relaxes. The four women loosen their grip. Their hands slowly caress his body.

The man leans forward again, kissing his cheek.

"Quetz!" he says, his voice cracking. His vision travels from woman to woman—the old familiar man, too. Tears run down cheeks. He remembers.

"Yes!" he whispers, his breath full of mirth and pain. They hear him. They understand.

A glimmer of light on the knife.

A flower.

A hummingbird takes flight.

About the Author

Grogan Ullah Khan lives with his wife, three dogs, seven cats, one horse, two donkeys , numerous fish, ghosts, spirts and jinn somewhere in the borderlands of Germakistan. He is an instructor of philosophy at a liberal arts college, and a senior manager at a non-profit organization. His master's thesis, entitled, "The Birth of Mexico: The Story of the Aztecs," is currently available through UMI, and is soon to be published.

Bibliography

Arbuthnot, Nancy. *Mexico Shining: Songs of the Aztecs.* Colorado: Three Continents Press, 1995.

0-595-21980-2

Printed in the United States
46696LVS00004B/42

9 780595 219803